Penguin Books
Jeeves in the Offing

Pelham Grenville Wodehouse was born in 1881 in Guildford, the son of a civil servant, and educated at Dulwich College. He spent a brief period working for the Hong Kong and Shanghai Bank before abandoning finance for writing, earning a living by journalism and selling stories to magazines.

An enormously popular and prolific writer, he produced about a hundred books. In Jeeves, the ever resourceful 'gentleman's personal gentleman', and the good-hearted young blunderer Bertie Wooster, he created two of the best-known and best-loved characters in twentieth-century literature. Their exploits, first collected in *Carry on, Jeeves*, were chronicled in fourteen books, and have been repeatedly adapted for television, radio and the stage. Wodehouse also created many other comic figures, notably Lord Emsworth, the Hon. Galahad Threepwood, Psmith and the numerous members of the Drones Club. He was part-author and writer of fifteen straight plays and of 250 lyrics for some thirty musical comedies. *The Times* hailed him as a 'comic genius recognized in his lifetime as a classic and an old master of farce'.

P. G. Wodehouse said, 'I believe there are two ways of writing novels. One is mine, making a sort of musical comedy without music and ignoring real life altogether; the other is going right deep down into life and not caring a damn.'

Wodehouse married in 1914 and took American citizenship in 1955. He was created a Knight of the British Empire in the 1975 New Year's Honours List. In a BBC interview he said that he had no ambitions left now that he had been knighted and there was a waxwork of him in Madame Tussaud's. He died on St Valentine's Day, 1975, at the age of ninety-three.

P. G. Wodehouse in Penguin

P. G. Wodehouse
Jeeves in the Offing

P. G. Wodehouse

Jeeves
in
the
Offing

PENGUIN BOOKS

PENGUIN BOOKS

Published by the Penguin Group
Penguin Books Ltd, 80 Strand, London WC2R 0RL, England
Penguin Putnam Inc., 375 Hudson Street, New York, New York 10014, USA
Penguin Books Australia Ltd, 250 Camberwell Road, Camberwell, Victoria 3124, Australia
Penguin Books Canada Ltd, 10 Alcorn Avenue, Toronto, Ontario, Canada M4V 3B2
Penguin Books India (P) Ltd, 11 Community Centre, Panchsheel Park, New Delhi – 110 017, India
Penguin Books (NZ) Ltd, Cnr Rosedale and Airborne Roads, Albany, Auckland, New Zealand
Penguin Books (South Africa) (Pty) Ltd, 24 Sturdee Avenue, Rosebank 2196, South Africa

Penguin Books Ltd, Registered Offices: 80 Strand, London WC2R 0RL, England

www.penguin.com

First published in Great Britain by Herbert Jenkins Ltd 1960
Published in Penguin Books 1963
25

Set in 9/11pt Monotype Trump
Typeset by Rowland Phototypesetting Ltd,
Bury St Edmunds, Suffolk
Printed in England by Clays Ltd, St Ives plc

I

Jeeves placed the sizzling eggs and b. on the breakfast table, and Reginald ('Kipper') Herring and I, licking the lips, squared our elbows and got down to it. A lifelong buddy of mine, this Herring, linked to me by what are called imperishable memories. Years ago, when striplings, he and I had done a stretch together at Malvern House, Bramley-on-Sea, the preparatory school conducted by that prince of stinkers, Aubrey Upjohn MA, and had frequently stood side by side in the Upjohn study awaiting the receipt of six of the juiciest from a cane of the type that biteth like a serpent and stingeth like an adder, as the fellow said. So we were, you might say, rather like a couple of old sweats who had fought shoulder to shoulder on Crispin's Day, if I've got the name right.

The *plat du jour* having gone down the hatch, accompanied by some fluid ounces of strengthening coffee, I was about to reach for the marmalade, when I heard the telephone tootling out in the hall and rose to attend to it.

'Bertram Wooster's residence,' I said, having connected with the instrument. 'Wooster in person at this end. Oh hullo,' I added, for the voice that boomed over the wire was that of Mrs Thomas Portarlington Travers of Brinkley Court, Market Snodsbury, near Droitwich – or, putting it another way, my good and deserving Aunt Dahlia. 'A very hearty pip-pip to you, old ancestor,' I said, well pleased, for she is a woman with whom it is always a privilege to chew the fat.

'And a rousing toodle-oo to you, you young blot on

the landscape,' she replied cordially. 'I'm surprised to
find you up as early as this. Or have you just got in from
a night on the tiles?'

I hastened to rebut this slur.

'Certainly not. Nothing of that description
whatsoever. I've been upping with the lark this last
week, to keep Kipper Herring company. He's staying
with me till he can get into his new flat. You remember
old Kipper? I brought him down to Brinkley one
summer. Chap with a cauliflower ear.'

'I know who you mean. Looks like Jack Dempsey.'

'That's right. Far more, indeed, than Jack Dempsey
does. He's on the staff of the *Thursday Review*, a
periodical of which you may or may not be a reader, and
has to clock in at the office at daybreak. No doubt, when
I apprise him of your call, he will send you his love, for I
know he holds you in high esteem. The perfect hostess,
he often describes you as. Well, it's nice to hear your
voice again, old flesh-and-blood. How's everything down
Market Snodsbury way?'

'Oh, we're jogging along. But I'm not speaking from
Brinkley. I'm in London.'

'Till when?'

'Driving back this afternoon.'

'I'll give you lunch.'

'Sorry, can't manage it. I'm putting on the nosebag
with Sir Roderick Glossop.'

This surprised me. The eminent brain specialist to
whom she alluded was a man I would not have cared to
lunch with myself, our relations having been on the stiff
side since the night at Lady Wickham's place in
Hertfordshire when, acting on the advice of my hostess's
daughter Roberta, I had punctured his hot-water bottle
with a darning needle in the small hours of the morning.
Quite unintentional, of course. I had planned to
puncture the h-w-b of his nephew Tuppy Glossop, with
whom I had a feud on, and unknown to me they had

changed rooms. Just one of those unfortunate misunderstandings.

'What on earth are you doing that for?'

'Why shouldn't I? He's paying.'

I saw her point – a penny saved is a penny earned and all that sort of thing – but I continued surprised. It amazed me that Aunt Dahlia, presumably a free agent, should have selected this very formidable loony-doctor to chew the mid-day chop with. However, one of the first lessons life teaches us is that aunts will be aunts, so I merely shrugged a couple of shoulders.

'Well, it's up to you, of course, but it seems a rash act. Did you come to London just to revel with Glossop?'

'No, I'm here to collect my new butler and take him home with me.'

'New butler? What's become of Seppings?'

'He's gone.'

I clicked the tongue. I was very fond of the major-domo in question, having enjoyed many a port in his pantry, and this news saddened me.

'No, really?' I said. 'Too bad. I thought he looked a little frail when I last saw him. Well, that's how it goes. All flesh is grass, I often say.'

'To Bognor Regis, for his holiday.'

I unclicked the tongue.

'Oh, I see. That puts a different complexion on the matter. Odd how all these pillars of the home seem to be dashing away on toots these days. It's like what Jeeves was telling me about the great race movements of the Middle Ages. Jeeves starts his holiday this morning. He's off to Herne Bay for the shrimping, and I'm feeling like that bird in the poem who lost his pet gazelle or whatever the animal was. I don't know what I'm going to do without him.'

'I'll tell you what you're going to do. Have you a clean shirt?'

'Several.'

3

'And a toothbrush?'

'Two, both of the finest quality.'

'Then pack them. You're coming to Brinkley tomorrow.'

The gloom which always envelops Bertram Wooster like a fog when Jeeves is about to take his annual vacation lightened perceptibly. There are few things I find more agreeable than a sojourn at Aunt Dahlia's rural lair. Picturesque scenery, gravel soil, main drainage, company's own water and, above all, the superb French cheffing of her French chef Anatole, God's gift to the gastric juices. A full hand, as you might put it.

'What an admirable suggestion,' I said. 'You solve all my problems and bring the blue bird out of a hat. Rely on me. You will observe me bowling up in the Wooster sports model tomorrow afternoon with my hair in a braid and a song on my lips. My presence will, I feel sure, stimulate Anatole to new heights of endeavour. Got anybody else staying at the old snake pit?'

'Five inmates in all.'

'Five?' I resumed my tongue-clicking. 'Golly! Uncle Tom must be frothing at the mouth a bit,' I said, for I knew the old buster's distaste for guests in the home. Even a single weekender is sometimes enough to make him drain the bitter cup.

'Tom's not there. He's gone to Harrogate with Cream.'

'You mean lumbago.'

'I don't mean lumbago. I mean Cream. Homer Cream. Big American tycoon, who is visiting these shores. He suffers from ulcers, and his medicine man has ordered him to take the waters at Harrogate. Tom has gone with him to hold his hand and listen to him of an evening while he tells him how filthy the stuff tastes.'

'Antagonistic.'

'What?'

'I mean altruistic. You are probably not familiar with the word, but it's one I've heard Jeeves use. It's what you say of a fellow who gives selfless service, not counting the cost.'

'Selfless service, my foot! Tom's in the middle of a very important business deal with Cream. If it goes through, he'll make a packet free of income tax. So he's sucking up to him like a Hollywood Yes-man.'

I gave an intelligent nod, though this of course was wasted on her because she couldn't see me. I could readily understand my uncle-by-marriage's mental processes. T. Portarlington Travers is a man who has accumulated the pieces of eight in sackfuls, but he is always more than willing to shove a bit extra away behind the brick in the fireplace, feeling – and rightly – that every little bit added to what you've got makes just a little bit more. And if there's one thing that's right up his street, it is not paying income tax. He grudges every penny the Government nicks him for.

'That is why, when kissing me goodbye, he urged me with tears in his eyes to lush Mrs Cream and her son Willie up and treat them like royalty. So they're at Brinkley, dug into the woodwork.'

'Willie, did you say?'

'Short for Wilbert.'

I mused. Willie Cream. The name seemed familiar somehow. I seemed to have heard it or seen it in the papers somewhere. But it eluded me.

'Adela Cream writes mystery stories. Are you a fan of hers? No? Well, start boning up on them, directly you arrive, because every little helps. I've bought a complete set. They're very good.'

'I shall be delighted to run an eye over her material,' I said, for I am what they call an a-something of novels of suspense. Aficionado, would that be it? 'I can always do with another corpse or two. We have established, then, that among the inmates are this Mrs Cream and her son Wilbert. Who are the other three?'

'Well, there's Lady Wickham's daughter Roberta.'

I started violently, as if some unseen hand had goosed me.

'What! Bobbie Wickham? Oh, my gosh!'

'Why the agitation? Do you know her?'

'You bet I know her.'

'I begin to see. Is she one of the gaggle of girls you've been engaged to?'

'Not actually, no. We were never engaged. But that was merely because she wouldn't meet me half-way.'

'Turned you down, did she?'

'Yes, thank goodness.'

'Why thank goodness? She's a one-girl beauty chorus.'

'She doesn't try the eyes, I agree.'

'A pippin, if ever there was one.'

'Very true, but is being a pippin everything? What price the soul?'

'Isn't her soul like mother makes?'

'Far from it. Much below par. What I could tell you . . . But no, let it go. Painful subj.'

I had been about to mention fifty-seven or so of the reasons why the prudent operator, if he valued his peace of mind, deemed it best to stay well away from the red-headed menace under advisement, but realized that at a moment when I was wanting to get back to the marmalade it would occupy too much time. It will be enough to say that I had long since come out of the ether and was fully cognizant of the fact that in declining to fall in with my suggestion that we should start rounding up clergymen and bridesmaids, the beasel had rendered me a signal service, and I'll tell you why.

Aunt Dahlia, describing this young blister as a one-girl beauty chorus, had called her shots perfectly correctly. Her outer crust was indeed of a nature to cause those beholding it to rock back on their heels with a startled whistle. But while equipped with eyes like twin stars, hair ruddier than the cherry, oomph, *espièglerie* and all the fixings, B. Wickham had also the disposition and general outlook on life of a ticking bomb. In her society you always had the uneasy feeling that something was likely to go off at any moment with a pop. You never knew what she was going to do next or into what murky depths of soup she would carelessly plunge you.

'Miss Wickham, sir,' Jeeves had once said to me warningly at the time when the fever was at its height, 'lacks seriousness. She is volatile and frivolous. I would always hesitate to recommend as a life partner a young lady with quite such a vivid shade of red hair.'

His judgment was sound. I have already mentioned how with her subtle wiles this girl had induced me to sneak into Sir Roderick Glossop's sleeping apartment and apply the darning needle to his hot-water bottle, and that was comparatively mild going for her. In a word, Roberta, daughter of the late Sir Cuthbert and Lady Wickham of Skeldings Hall, Herts, was pure dynamite and better kept at a distance by all those who aimed at leading the peaceful life. The prospect of being immured with her in the same house, with all the facilities a country-house affords an enterprising girl for landing her nearest and dearest in the mulligatawny, made me singularly dubious about the shape of things to come.

And I was tottering under this blow when the old relative administered another, and it was a haymaker.

'And there's Aubrey Upjohn and his stepdaughter Phyllis Mills,' she said. 'That's the lot. What's the matter with you? Got asthma?'

I took her to be alluding to the sharp gasp which had escaped my lips, and I must confess that it had come out not unlike the last words of a dying duck. But I felt perfectly justified in gasping. A weaker man would have howled like a banshee. There floated into my mind something Kipper Herring had once said to me. 'You know, Bertie,' he had said, in philosophical mood, 'we have much to be thankful for in this life of ours, you and I. However rough the going, there is one sustaining thought to which we can hold. The storm clouds may lower and the horizon grow dark, we may get a nail in our shoe and be caught in the rain without an umbrella, we may come down to breakfast and find that someone else has taken the brown egg, but at least we have the consolation of knowing that we shall never see Aubrey Gawd-help-us Upjohn again. Always remember this in times of despondency,' he said, and I always had. And now here the bounder was, bobbing up right in my midst. Enough to make the stoutest-hearted go into his dying-duck routine.

'Aubrey Upjohn?' I quavered. 'You mean *my* Aubrey Upjohn?'

'That's the one. Soon after you made your escape from his chain gang he married Jane Mills, a friend of mine with a colossal amount of money. She died, leaving a daughter. I'm the daughter's godmother. Upjohn's retired now and going in for politics. The hot tip is that the boys in the back room are going to run him as the Conservative candidate in the Market Snodsbury division at the next by-election. What a thrill it'll be for you, meeting him again. Or does the prospect scare you?'

'Certainly not. We Woosters are intrepid. But what on earth did you invite him to Brinkley for?'

'I didn't. I only wanted Phyllis, but he came along, too.'

'You should have bunged him out.'

'I hadn't the heart to.'

'Weak, very weak.'

'Besides, I needed him in my business. He's going to present the prizes at Market Snodsbury Grammar School. We've been caught short as usual, and somebody has got to make a speech on ideals and the great world outside to those blasted boys, so he fits in nicely. I believe he's a very fine speaker. His only trouble is that he's stymied unless he has his speech with him and can read it. Calls it referring to his notes. Phyllis told me that. She types the stuff for him.'

'A thoroughly low trick,' I said severely. 'Even I, who have never soared above the Yeoman's Wedding Song at a village concert, wouldn't have the crust to face my public unless I'd taken the trouble to memorize the words, though actually with the Yeoman's Wedding Song it is possible to get by quite comfortably by keeping singing "Ding dong, ding dong, ding dong, I hurry along". In short . . .'

I would have spoken further, but at this point, after urging me to put a sock in it, and giving me a kindly word of warning not to step on any banana skins, she rang off.

2

I came away from the telephone on what practically amounted to leaden feet. Here, I was feeling, was a nice bit of box fruit. Bobbie Wickham, with her tendency to stir things up and with each new day to discover some new way of staggering civilization, would by herself have been bad enough. Add Aubrey Upjohn, and the mixture became too rich. I don't know if Kipper, when I rejoined him, noticed that my brow was sicklied o'er with the pale cast of thought, as I have heard Jeeves put it. Probably not, for he was tucking into toast and marmalade at the moment, but it was. As had happened so often in the past, I was conscious of an impending doom. Exactly what form this would take I was of course unable to say – it might be one thing or it might be another – but a voice seemed to whisper to me that somehow at some not distant date Bertram was slated to get it in the gizzard.

'That was Aunt Dahlia, Kipper,' I said.

'Bless her jolly old heart,' he responded. 'One of the very best, and you can quote me as saying so. I shall never forget those happy days at Brinkley, and shall be glad at any time that suits her to cadge another invitation. Is she up in London?'

'Till this afternoon.'

'We fill her to the brim with rich foods, of course?'

'No, she's got a lunch date. She's browsing with Sir Roderick Glossop, the loony-doctor. You don't know him, do you?'

'Only from hearing you speak of him. A tough egg, I gather.'

'One of the toughest.'

'He was the chap, wasn't he, who found the twenty-four cats in your bedroom?'

'Twenty-three,' I corrected. I like to get things right. 'They were not my cats. They had been deposited there by my Cousins Claude and Eustace. But I found them difficult to explain. He's a rather bad listener. I hope I shan't find him at Brinkley, too.'

'Are you going to Brinkley?'

'Tomorrow afternoon.'

'You'll enjoy that.'

'Well, shall I? The point is a very moot one.'

'You're crazy. Think of Anatole. Those dinners of his! Is the name of the Peri who stood disconsolate at the gate of Eden familiar to you?'

'I've heard Jeeves mention her.'

'Well, that's how I feel when I remember Anatole's dinners. When I reflect that every night he's dishing them up and I'm not there, I come within a very little of breaking down. What gives you the idea that you won't enjoy yourself? Brinkley Court's an earthly Paradise.'

'In many respects, yes, but life there at the moment has its drawbacks. There's far too much of that where-every-prospect-pleases-and-only-man-is-vile stuff buzzing around for my taste. Who do you think is staying at the old dosshouse? Aubrey Upjohn.'

It was plain that I had shaken him. His eyes widened, and an astonished piece of toast fell from his grasp.

'Old Upjohn? You're kidding.'

'No, he's there. Himself, not a picture. And it seems only yesterday that you were buoying me up by telling me I'd never have to see him again. The storm clouds may lower, you said, if you recollect . . .'

'But how does he come to be at Brinkley?'

'Precisely what I asked the aged relative, and she had an explanation that seems to cover the facts. Apparently after we took our eye off him he married a friend of hers, one Jane Mills, and acquired a stepdaughter, Phyllis Mills, whose godmother Aunt Dahlia is. The ancestor invited the Mills girl to Brinkley, and Upjohn came along for the ride.'

'I see. I don't wonder you're trembling like a leaf.'

'Not like a leaf, exactly, but . . . yes, I think you might describe me as trembling. One remembers that fishy eye of his.'

'And the wide, bare upper lip. It won't be pleasant having to gaze at those across the dinner table. Still, you'll like Phyllis.'

'Do you know her?'

'We met out in Switzerland last Christmas. Slap her on the back, will you, and give her my regards. Nice girl, though goofy. She never told me she was related to Upjohn.'

'She would naturally keep a thing like that dark.'

'Yes, one sees that. Just as one would have tried to keep it dark if one had been mixed up in any way with Palmer the poisoner. What ghastly garbage that was he used to fling at us when we were serving our sentence at Malvern House. Remember the sausages on Sunday? And the boiled mutton with caper sauce?'

'And the margarine. Recalling this last, it's going to be a strain having to sit and watch him getting outside pounds of best country butter. Oh, Jeeves,' I said, as he shimmered in to clear the table, 'you never went to a preparatory school on the south coast of England, did you?'

'No, sir, I was privately educated.'

'Ah, then you wouldn't understand. Mr Herring and I were discussing our former prep-school beak, Aubrey Upjohn, MA. By the way, Kipper, Aunt Dahlia was telling me something about him which I never knew before and which ought to expose him to the odium of all thinking men. You remember those powerful end-of-term addresses he used to make to us? Well, he

couldn't have made them if he hadn't had the stuff all
typed out in his grasp, so that he could read it. Without
his notes, as he calls them, he's a spent force. Revolting,
that, Jeeves, don't you think?'

'Many orators are, I believe, similarly handicapped,
sir.'

'Too tolerant, Jeeves, far too tolerant. You must guard
against this lax outlook. However, the reason I mention
Upjohn to you is that he has come back into my life, or
will be so coming in about two ticks. He's staying at
Brinkley, and I shall be going there tomorrow. That was
Aunt Dahlia on the phone just now, and she demands
my presence. Will you pack a few necessaries in a
suitcase or so?'

'Very good, sir.'

'When are you leaving on your Herne Bay jaunt?'

'I was thinking of taking a train this morning, sir, but
if you would prefer that I remained till tomorrow – '

'No, no, perfectly all right. Start as soon as you like.
What's the joke?' I asked, as the door closed behind him,
for I observed that Kipper was chuckling softly. Not an
easy thing to do, of course, when your mouth's full of
toast and marmalade, but he was doing it.

'I was thinking of Upjohn,' he said.

I was amazed. It seemed incredible to me that anyone
who had done time at Malvern House, Bramley-on-Sea,
could chuckle, softly or otherwise, when letting the
mind dwell on that outstanding menace. It was like
laughing lightly while contemplating one of those
horrors from outer space which are so much with us at
the moment on the motion-picture screen.

'I envy you, Bertie,' he went on, continuing to
chuckle. 'You have a wonderful treat in store. You are
going to be present at the breakfast table when Upjohn
opens his copy of this week's *Thursday Review* and
starts to skim through the pages devoted to comments
on current literature. I should explain that among the

books that recently arrived at the office was a slim volume from his pen dealing with the Preparatory School and giving it an enthusiastic build-up. The formative years which we spent there, he said, were the happiest of our life.'

'Gadzooks!'

'He little knew that his brain child would be given to one of the old lags of Malvern House to review. I'll tell you something, Bertie, that every young man ought to know. Never be a stinker, because if you are, though you may flourish for a time like a green bay tree, sooner or later retribution will overtake you. I need scarcely tell you that I ripped the stuffing out of the beastly little brochure. The thought of those sausages on Sunday filled me with the righteous fury of a Juvenal.'

'Of a who?'

'Nobody you know. Before your time. I seemed inspired. Normally, I suppose, a book like that would get me a line and a half in the Other Recent Publications column, but I gave it six hundred words of impassioned prose. How extraordinarily fortunate you are to be in a position to watch his face as he reads them.'

'How do you know he'll read them?'

'He's a subscriber. There was a letter from him on the correspondence page a week or two ago, in which he specifically stated that he had been one for years.'

'Did you sign the thing?'

'No. Ye Ed is not keen on underlings advertising their names.'

'And it was really hot stuff?'

'Red hot. So eye him closely at the breakfast table. Mark his reaction. I confidently expect the blush of shame and remorse to mantle his cheek.'

'The only catch is that I don't come down to breakfast when I'm at Brinkley. Still, I suppose I could make a special effort.'

'Do so. You will find it well worth while,' said Kipper

and shortly afterwards popped off to resume the earning
of the weekly envelope.

He had been gone about twenty minutes when Jeeves
came in, bowler hat in hand, to say goodbye. A solemn
moment, taxing our self-control to the utmost.
However, we both kept the upper lip stiff, and after we
had kidded back and forth for a while he started to
withdraw. He had reached the door when it suddenly
occurred to me that he might have inside information
about this Wilbert Cream of whom Aunt Dahlia had
spoken. I have generally found that he knows everything
about everyone.

'Oh, Jeeves,' I said. 'Half a jiffy.'

'Sir?'

'Something I want to ask you. It seems that among
my fellow-guests at Brinkley will be a Mrs Homer
Cream, wife of an American big butter and egg man, and
her son Wilbert, commonly known as Willie, and the
name Willie Cream seemed somehow to touch a chord.
Rightly or wrongly I associate it with trips we have
taken to New York, but in what connection I haven't
the vaguest. Does it ring a bell with you?'

'Why yes, sir. References to the gentleman are
frequent in the tabloid newspapers of New York, notably
in the column conducted by Mr Walter Winchell. He is
generally alluded to under the sobriquet of Broadway
Willie.'

'Of course! It all comes back to me. He's what they
call a playboy.'

'Precisely, sir. Notorious for his escapades.'

'Yes, I've got him placed now. He's the fellow who
likes to let off stink bombs in night clubs, which rather
falls under the head of carrying coals to Newcastle, and
seldom cashes a cheque at his bank without producing a
gat and saying, "This is a stick-up." '

'And . . . No, sir, I regret that it has for the moment
escaped my memory.'

'What has?'

'Some other little something, sir, that I was told regarding Mr Cream. Should I recall it, I will communicate with you.'

'Yes, do. One wants the complete picture. Oh, gosh!'

'Sir?'

'Nothing, Jeeves. Just a thought has floated into my mind. All right, push off, or you'll miss your train. Good luck to your shrimping net.'

I'll tell you what the thought was that had floated. I have already indicated my qualms at the prospect of being cooped up in the same house with Bobbie Wickham and Aubrey Upjohn, for who could tell what the harvest might be? If in addition to these two heavies I was also to be cheek by jowl with a New York playboy apparently afflicted with bats in the belfry, it began to look as if this visit would prove too much for Bertram's frail strength, and for an instant I toyed with the idea of sending a telegram of regret and oiling out.

Then I remembered Anatole's cooking and was strong again. Nobody who has once tasted them would wantonly deprive himself of that wizard's smoked offerings. Whatever spiritual agonies I might be about to undergo at Brinkley Court, Market Snodsbury, near Droitwich, residence there would at least put me several *Suprêmes de fois gras au champagne* and *Mignonettes de Poulet Petit Duc* ahead of the game. Nevertheless, it would be paltering with the truth to say that I was at my ease as I thought of what lay before me in darkest Worcestershire, and the hand that lit the after-breakfast gasper shook quite a bit.

At this moment of nervous tension the telephone suddenly gave tongue again, causing me to skip like the high hills, as if the Last Trump had sounded. I went to the instrument all of a twitter.

Some species of butler appeared to be at the other end.

'Mr Wooster?'

'On the spot.'

'Good morning, sir. Her ladyship wishes to speak to you. Lady Wickham, sir. Here is Mr Wooster, m'lady.'

And Bobbie's mother came on the air.

I should have mentioned, by the way, that during the above exchange of ideas with the butler I had been aware of a distant sound of sobbing, like background music, and it now became apparent that it was from the larynx of the relict of the late Sir Cuthbert that it was proceeding. There was a short intermission before she got the vocal cords working, and while I was waiting for her to start the dialogue I found myself wrestling with two problems that presented themselves – the first, What on earth is this woman ringing me up for?, the second, Having got the number, why does she sob?

It was Problem A that puzzled me particularly, for ever since that hot-water-bottle episode my relations with this parent of Bobbie's had been on the strained side. It was, indeed, an open secret that my standing with her was practically that of a rat of the underworld. I had had this from Bobbie, whose impersonation of her mother discussing me with sympathetic cronies had been exceptionally vivid, and I must confess that I wasn't altogether surprised. No hostess, I mean to say, extending her hospitality to a friend of her daughter's, likes to have the young visitor going about the place puncturing people's water-bottles and leaving at three in the morning without stopping to say good-bye. Yes, I could see her side of the thing all right, and I found it extraordinary that she should be seeking me out on the telephone in this fashion. Feeling as she did so allergic to Bertram, I wouldn't have thought she'd have phoned me with a ten-foot pole.

However, there beyond a question she was.

'Mr Wooster?'

'Oh, hullo, Lady Wickham.'

'Are you there?'

I put her straight on this point, and she took time out to sob again. She then spoke in a hoarse, throaty voice, like Tallulah Bankhead after swallowing a fish bone the wrong way.

'Is this awful news true?'

'Eh?'

'Oh dear, oh dear, oh dear!'

'I don't quite follow.'

'In this morning's *Times*.'

I'm pretty shrewd, and it seemed to me, reading between the lines, that there must have been something in the issue of *The Times* published that morning that for some reason had upset her, though why she should have chosen me to tell her troubles to was a mystery not easy to fathom. I was about to institute inquiries in the hope of spearing a solution, when in addition to sobbing she started laughing in a hyaena-esque manner, making it clear to my trained ear that she was having hysterics. And before I could speak there was a dull thud suggestive of some solid body falling to earth, I knew not where, and when the dialogue was resumed, I found that the butler had put himself on as an understudy.

'Mr Wooster?'

'Still here.'

'I regret to say that her ladyship has fainted.'

'It was she I heard going bump?'

'Precisely, sir. Thank you very much, sir. Good-bye.'

He replaced the receiver and went about his domestic duties, these no doubt including the loosening of the stricken woman's corsets and burning feathers under her nose, leaving me to chew on the situation without further bulletins from the front.

It seemed to me that the thing to do here was to get hold of *The Times* and see what it had to offer in the way of enlightenment. It's a paper I don't often look at, preferring for breakfast reading the *Mirror* and the *Mail*, but Jeeves takes it in and I have occasionally borrowed his copy with a view to having a shot at the crossword puzzle. It struck me as a possibility that he might have left today's issue in the kitchen, and so it proved. I came back with it, lowered myself into a chair, lit another cigarette and proceeded to cast an eye on its contents.

At a cursory glance what might be called swoon material appeared to be totally absent from its columns. The Duchess of something had been opening a bazaar at Wimbledon in aid of a deserving charity, there was an article on salmon fishing on the Wye, and a Cabinet Minister had made a speech about conditions in the cotton industry, but I could see nothing in these items to induce a loss of consciousness. Nor did it seem probable that a woman would have passed out cold on reading that Herbert Robinson (26) of Grove Road, Ponder's End, had been jugged for stealing a pair of green and yellow checked trousers. I turned to the cricket news. Had some friend of hers failed to score in one of yesterday's county matches owing to a doubtful l.b.w. decision?

It was just after I had run the eye down the Births and Marriages that I happened to look at the Engagements, and a moment later I was shooting out of my chair as if a spike had come through its cushioned seat and penetrated the fleshy parts.

'Jeeves!' I yelled, and then remembered that he had long since gone with the wind. A bitter thought, for if ever there was an occasion when his advice and counsel were of the essence, this occ. was that occ. The best I could do, tackling it solo, was to utter a hollow g. and bury the face in the hands. And though I seem to hear my public tut-tutting in disapproval of such neurotic behaviour, I think the verdict of history will be that the paragraph on which my gaze had rested was more than enough to excuse a spot of face-burying.

It ran as follows:

FORTHCOMING MARRIAGES

The engagement is announced between Bertram
Wilberforce Wooster of Berkeley Mansions, W.1, and
Roberta, daughter of the late Sir Cuthbert Wickham
and Lady Wickham of Skeldings Hall, Herts.

3

Well, as I was saying, I had several times when under the influence of her oomph taken up with Roberta Wickham the idea of such a merger, but – and here is the point I would stress – I could have sworn that on each occasion she had declined to co-operate, and that in a manner which left no room for doubt regarding her views. I mean to say, when a girl, offered a good man's heart, laughs like a bursting paper bag and tells him not to be a silly ass, the good man is entitled, I think, to assume that the whole thing is off. In the light of this announcement in *The Times* I could only suppose that on one of these occasions, unnoticed by me possibly because my attention had wandered, she must have drooped her eyes and come through with a murmured 'Right-ho.' Though when this could have happened, I hadn't the foggiest.

It was, accordingly, as you will readily imagine, a Bertram Wooster with dark circles under his eyes and a brain threatening to come apart at the seams who braked the sports model on the following afternoon at the front door of Brinkley Court – a Bertram, in a word, who was asking himself what the dickens all this was about. Non-plussed more or less sums it up. It seemed to me that my first move must be to get hold of my fiancée and see if she had anything to contribute in the way of clarifying the situation.

As is generally the case at country-houses on a fine day, there seemed to be nobody around. In due season the gang would assemble for tea on the lawn, but at the moment I could spot no friendly native to tell me where

I might find Bobbie. I proceeded, therefore, to roam
hither and thither about the grounds and messuages in
the hope of locating her, wishing that I had a couple of
bloodhounds to aid me in my task, for the Travers
demesne is a spacious one and there was a considerable
amount of sunshine above, though none, I need scarcely
mention, in my heart.

And I was tooling along a mossy path with the brow a
bit wet with honest sweat, when there came to my ears
the unmistakable sound of somebody reading poetry to
someone, and the next moment I found myself
confronting a mixed twosome who had dropped anchor
beneath a shady tree in what is known as a leafy glade.

They had scarcely swum into my ken when the
welkin started ringing like billy-o. This was due to the
barking of a small dachshund, who now advanced on me
with the apparent intention of seeing the colour of my
insides. Milder counsels, however, prevailed, and on
arriving at journey's end he merely rose like a rocket and
licked me on the chin, seeming to convey the
impression that in Bertram Wooster he had found just
what the doctor ordered. I have noticed before in dogs
this tendency to form a beautiful friendship immediately
on getting within sniffing distance of me. Something to
do, no doubt, with the characteristic Wooster smell,
which for some reason seems to speak to their deeps. I
tickled him behind the right ear and scratched the base
of his spine for a moment or two: then, these civilities
concluded, switched my attention to the poetry group.

It was the male half of the sketch who had been doing
the reading, a willowy bird of about the tonnage and
general aspect of David Niven with ginger hair and a
small moustache. As he was unquestionably not Aubrey
Upjohn, I assumed that this must be Willie Cream, and
it surprised me a bit to find him dishing out verse. One
would have expected a New York playboy, widely
publicized as one of the lads, to confine himself to prose,

and dirty prose, at that. But no doubt these playboys have their softer moments.

His companion was a well-stacked young featherweight, who could be none other than the Phyllis Mills of whom Kipper had spoken. Nice but goofy, Kipper had said, and a glance told me that he was right. One learns, as one goes through life, to spot goofiness in the other sex with an unerring eye, and this exhibit had a sort of mild, Soul's Awakening kind of expression which made it abundantly clear that, while not a super-goof like some of the female goofs I'd met, she was quite goofy enough to be going on with. Her whole aspect was that of a girl who at the drop of a hat would start talking baby talk.

This she now proceeded to do, asking me if I didn't think that Poppet, the dachshund, was a sweet little doggie. I assented rather austerely, for I prefer the shorter form more generally used, and she said she supposed I was Mrs Travers's nephew Bertie Wooster, which, as we knew, was substantially the case.

'I heard you were expected today. I'm Phyllis Mills,' she said, and I said I had divined as much and that Kipper had told me to slap her on the back and give her his best, and she said, 'Oh, Reggie Herring? He's a sweetie-pie, isn't he?' and I agreed that Kipper was one of the sweetie-pies and not the worst of them, and she said, 'Yes, he's a lambkin.'

This duologue had, of course, left Wilbert Cream a bit out of it, just painted on the backdrop as you might say, and for some moments, knitting his brow, plucking at his moustache, shuffling the feet and allowing the limbs to twitch, he had been giving abundant evidence that in his opinion three was a crowd and that what the leafy glade needed to make it all that a leafy glade should be was a complete absence of Woosters. Taking advantage of a lull in the conversation, he said:

'Are you looking for someone?'

I replied that I was looking for Bobbie Wickham.

'I'd go on looking, if I were you. Bound to find her somewhere.'

'Bobbie?' said Phyllis Mills. 'She's down at the lake, fishing.'

'Then what you do,' said Wilbert Cream, brightening, 'is follow this path, bend right, sharp left, bend right again and there you are. You can't miss. Start at once, is my advice.'

I must say I felt that, related as I was by ties of blood, in a manner of speaking, to this leafy glade, it was a bit thick being practically bounced from it by a mere visitor, but Aunt Dahlia had made it clear that the Cream family must not be thwarted or put upon in any way, so I did as he suggested, picking up the feet without anything in the nature of back chat. As I receded, I could hear in my rear the poetry breaking out again.

The lake at Brinkley calls itself a lake, but when all the returns are in it's really more a sort of young pond. Big enough to mess about on in a punt, though, and for the use of those wishing to punt a boat-house has been provided with a small pier or landing stage attached to it. On this, rod in hand, Bobbie was seated, and it was with me the work of an instant to race up and breathe down the back of her neck.

'Hey!' I said.

'Hey to you with knobs on,' she replied. 'Oh, hullo, Bertie. You here?'

'You never spoke a truer word. If you can spare me a moment of your valuable time, young Roberta –'

'Half a second, I think I've got a bite. No, false alarm. What were you saying?'

'I was saying –'

'Oh, by the way, I heard from Mother this morning.'

'I heard from her yesterday morning.'

'I was kind of expecting you would. You saw that thing in *The Times*?'

'With the naked eye.'

'Puzzled you for a moment, perhaps?'

'For several moments.'

'Well, I'll tell you all about that. The idea came to me in a flash.'

'You mean it was you who shoved that communiqué in the journal?'

'Of course.'

'Why?' I said, getting right down to it in my direct way.

I thought I had her there, but no.

'I was paving the way for Reggie.'

I passed a hand over my fevered brow.

'Something seems to have gone wrong with my usually keen hearing,' I said. 'It sounds just as if you were saying "I was paving the way for Reggie."'

'I was. I was making his path straight. Softening up Mother on his behalf.'

I passed another hand over my f.b.

'Now you seem to be saying "Softening up Mother on his behalf."'

'That's what I am saying. It's perfectly simple. I'll put it in words of one syllable for you. I love Reggie. Reggie loves me.'

'Reggie,' of course, is two syllables, but I let it go.

'Reggie who?'

'Reggie Herring.'

I was amazed.

'You mean old Kipper?'

'I wish you wouldn't call him Kipper.'

'I always have. Dash it,' I said with some warmth, 'if a fellow shows up at a private school on the south coast of England with a name like Herring, what else do you expect his playmates to call him? But how do you mean you love him and he loves you? You've never met him.'

'Of course I've met him. We were in the same hotel in Switzerland last Christmas. I taught him to ski,' she said, a dreamy look coming into her twin starlikes. 'I shall never forget the day I helped him unscramble himself after he had taken a toss on the beginners' slope. He had both legs wrapped round his neck. I think that is when love dawned. My heart melted as I sorted him out.'

'You didn't laugh?'

'Of course I didn't laugh. I was all sympathy and understanding.'

For the first time the thing began to seem plausible to me. Bobbie is a fun-loving girl, and the memory of her reaction when in the garden at Skeldings I had once stepped on the teeth of a rake and had the handle jump up and hit me on the tip of the nose was still laid away among my souvenirs. She had been convulsed with mirth. If, then, she had refrained from guffawing when confronted with the spectacle of Reginald Herring with both legs wrapped round his neck, her emotions must have been very deeply involved.

'Well, all right,' I said. 'I accept your statement that you and Kipper are that way. But why, that being so, did you blazon it forth to the world, if blazoning forth is the expression I want, that you were engaged to me?'

'I told you. It was to soften Mother up.'

'Which sounded to me like delirium straight from the sick bed.'

'You don't get the subtle strategy?'

'Not by several parasangs.'

'Well, you know how you stand with Mother.'

'Our relations are a bit distant.'

'She shudders at the mention of your name. So I thought if she thought I was going to marry you and then found I wasn't, she'd be so thankful for the merciful escape I'd had that she'd be ready to accept anyone as a son-in-law, even someone like Reggie, who, though a wonder man, hasn't got his name in Debrett and isn't any too hot financially. Mother's idea of a

mate for me has always been a well-to-do millionaire
or a Duke with a large private income. Now do you
follow?'

'Oh yes, I follow all right. You've been doing what
Jeeves does, studying the psychology of the individual.
But do you think it'll work?'

'Bound to. Let's take a parallel case. Suppose your
Aunt Dahlia read in the paper one morning that you
were going to be shot at sunrise.'

'I couldn't be. I'm never up so early.'

'But suppose she did? She'd be pretty worked up about
it, wouldn't she?'

'Extremely, one imagines, for she loves me dearly.
I'm not saying her manner toward me doesn't verge at
times on the brusque. In childhood days she would
occasionally clump me on the side of the head, and since
I have grown to riper years she has more than once
begged me to tie a brick around my neck and go and
drown myself in the pond in the kitchen garden.
Nevertheless, she loves her Bertram, and if she heard I
was to be shot at sunrise, she would, as you say, be as
sore as a gum-boil. But why? What's that got to do with
it?'

'Well, suppose she then found out it was all a mistake
and it wasn't you but somebody else who was to face the
firing squad. That would make her happy, wouldn't it?'

'One can picture her dancing all over the place on the
tips of her toes.'

'Exactly. She'd be so all over you that nothing you did
would be wrong in her eyes. Whatever you wanted to do
would be all right with her. Go to it, she would say. And
that's how Mother will feel when she learns that I'm not
marrying you after all. She'll be so relieved.'

I agreed that the relief would, of course, be
stupendous.

'But you'll be giving her the inside facts in a day or
two?' I said, for I was anxious to have assurance on this

point. A man with an Engagement notice in *The Times* hanging over him cannot but feel uneasy.

'Well, call it a week or two. No sense in rushing things.'

'You want me to sink in?'

'That's the idea.'

'And meanwhile what's the drill? Do I kiss you a good deal from time to time?'

'No, you don't.'

'Right-ho. I just want to know where I stand.'

'An occasional passionate glance will be ample.'

'It shall be attended to. Well, I'm delighted about you and Kipper or, as you would prefer to say, Reggie. There's nobody I'd rather see you centre-aisle-ing with.'

'It's very sporting of you to take it like this.'

'Don't give it a thought.'

'I'm awfully fond of you, Bertie.'

'Me, too, of you.'

'But I can't marry everybody, can I?'

'I wouldn't even try. Well, now that we've got all that straight, I suppose I'd better be going and saying "Come aboard" to Aunt Dahlia.'

'What's the time?'

'Close on five.'

'I must run like a hare. I'm supposed to be presiding at the tea table.'

'You? Why you?'

'Your aunt's not here. She found a telegram when she got back yesterday saying that her son Bonzo was sick of a fever at his school, and dashed off to be with him. She asked me to deputy-hostess for her till her return, but I shan't be able to for the next few days. I've got to dash back to Mother. Ever since she saw that thing in *The Times*, she's been wiring me every hour on the hour to come home for a round-table conference. What's a guffin?'

'I don't know. Why?'

'That's what she calls you in her latest 'gram. Quote.
"Cannot understand how you can be contemplating
marrying that guffin." Close quote. I suppose it's more
or less the same as a gaby, which was how you figured in
one of her earlier communications.'

'That sounds promising.'

'Yes, I think the thing's in the bag. After you, Reggie
will come to her like rare and refreshing fruit. She'll lay
down the red carpet for him.'

And with a brief 'Whoopee!' she shot off in the
direction of the house at forty or so m.p.h. I followed
more slowly, for she had given me much food for
thought, and I was musing.

Strange, I was feeling, this strong
pro-Kipper sentiment in the Wickham bosom. I mean,
consider the facts. What with that *espièglerie* of hers,
which was tops, she had been pretty extensively wooed
in one quarter and another for years, and no business had
resulted, so that it was generally assumed that only
something extra special in the way of suitors would
meet her specifications and that whoever eventually got
his nose under the wire would be a king among men and
pretty warm stuff. And she had gone and signed up with
Kipper Herring.

Mind you, I'm not saying a word against old Kipper.
The salt of the earth. But nobody could have called him
a knock-out in the way of looks. Having gone in a lot for
boxing from his earliest years, he had the cauliflower ear
of which I had spoken to Aunt Dahlia and in addition to
this a nose which some hidden hand had knocked
slightly out of the straight. He would, in short, have
been an unsafe entrant to have backed in a beauty
contest, even if the only other competitors had been
Boris Karloff, King Kong and Oofy Prosser of the Drones.

But then, of course, one had to remind oneself that
looks aren't everything. A cauliflower ear can hide a
heart of gold, as in Kipper's case it did, his being about as

gold as they come. His brain, too, might have helped to do the trick. You can't hold down an editorial post on an important London weekly paper without being fairly well fixed with the little grey cells, and girls admire that sort of thing. And one had to remember that most of the bimbos to whom Roberta Wickham had been giving the bird through the years had been of the huntin', shootin' and fishin' type, fellows who had more or less shot their bolt after saying 'Eh, what?' and slapping their leg with a hunting crop. Kipper must have come as a nice change.

Still, the whole thing provided, as I say, food for thought, and I was in what is called a reverie as I made my way to the house, a reverie so profound that no turf accountant would have given any but the shortest odds against my sooner or later bumping into something. And this, to cut a long story s., I did. It might have been a tree, a bush or a rustic seat. In actual fact it turned out to be Aubrey Upjohn. I came on him round a corner and rammed him squarely before I could put the brakes on. I clutched him round the neck and he clutched me about the middle, and for some moments we tottered to and fro, linked in a close embrace. Then, the mists clearing from my eyes, I saw who it was that I had been treading the measure with.

Seeing him steadily and seeing him whole, as I have heard Jeeves put it, I was immediately struck by the change that had taken place in his appearance since those get-togethers in his study at Malvern House, Bramley-on-Sea, when with a sinking heart I had watched him reach for the whangee and start limbering up the shoulder muscles with a few trial swings. At that period of our acquaintance he had been an upstanding old gentleman about eight feet six in height with burning eyes, foam-flecked lips and flame coming out of both nostrils. He had now shrunk to a modest five foot seven or there-abouts, and I could have felled him with a single blow.

Not that I did, of course. But I regarded him without a trace of the old trepidation. It seemed incredible that I could ever have considered this human shrimp a danger to pedestrians and traffic.

I think this was partly due to the fact that at some point in the fifteen years since our last meeting he had grown a moustache. In the Malvern House epoch what had always struck a chill into the plastic mind had been his wide, bare upper lip, a most unpleasant spectacle to behold, especially when twitching. I wouldn't say the moustache softened his face, but being of the walrus or soup-strainer type it hid some of it, which was all to the good. The up-shot was that instead of quailing, as I had expected to do when we met, I was suave and debonair, possibly a little too much so.

'Oh, hullo, Upjohn!' I said. 'Yoo-hoo!'

'Who you?' he responded, making it sound like a reverse echo.

'Wooster is the name.'

'Oh, Wooster?' he said, as if he had been hoping it would be something else, and one could understand his feelings, of course. No doubt he, like me, had been buoying himself up for years with the thought that we should never meet again and that, whatever brickbats life might have in store for him, he had at least got Bertram out of his system. A nasty jar it must have been for the poor bloke having me suddenly pop up from a trap like this.

'Long time since we met,' I said.

'Yes,' he agreed in a hollow voice, and it was so plain that he was wishing it had been longer that conversation flagged, and there wasn't much in the way of feasts of reason and flows of the soul as we covered the hundred yards to the lawn where the tea table awaited us. I think I may have said 'Nice day, what?' and he may have grunted, but nothing more.

Only Bobbie was present when we arrived at the

trough. Wilbert and Phyllis were presumably still in the leafy glade, and Mrs Cream, Bobbie said, worked in her room every afternoon on her new spine-freezer and seldom knocked off for a cuppa. We seated ourselves and had just started sipping, when the butler came out of the house bearing a bowl of fruit and hove to beside the table with it.

Well, when I say 'butler', I use the term loosely. He was dressed like a butler and he behaved like a butler, but in the deepest and truest sense of the word he was not a butler.

Reading from left to right, he was Sir Roderick Glossop.

4

At the Drones Club and other places I am accustomed to frequent you will often hear comment on Bertram Wooster's self-control or sang froid, as it's sometimes called, and it is generally agreed that this is considerable. In the eyes of many people, I suppose, I seem one of those men of chilled steel you read about, and I'm not saying I'm not. But it is possible to find a chink in my armour, and this can be done by suddenly springing eminent loony-doctors on me in the guise of butlers.

It was out of the q. that I could have been mistaken in supposing that it was Sir Roderick Glossop who, having delivered the fruit, was now ambling back to the house. There could not be two men with that vast bald head and those bushy eyebrows, and it would be deceiving the customers to say that I remained unshaken. The effect the apparition had on me was to make me start violently, and we all know what happens when you start violently while holding a full cup of tea. The contents of mine flew through the air and came to rest on the trousers of Aubrey Upjohn, MA, moistening them to no little extent. Indeed, it would scarcely be distorting the facts to say that he was now not so much wearing trousers as wearing tea.

I could see the unfortunate man felt his position deeply, and I was surprised that he contented himself with a mere 'Ouch!' But I suppose these solid citizens have to learn to curb the tongue. Creates a bad impression, I mean, if they start blinding and stiffing as those more happily placed would be.

But words are not always needed. In the look he now

shot at me I seemed to read a hundred unspoken expletives. It was the sort of look the bucko mate of a tramp steamer would have given an able-bodied seaman who for one reason or another had incurred his displeasure.

'I see you have not changed since you were with me at Malvern House,' he said in an extremely nasty voice, dabbing at the trousers with a handkerchief. 'Bungling Wooster we used to call him,' he went on, addressing his remarks to Bobbie and evidently trying to enlist her sympathy. 'He could not perform the simplest action such as holding a cup without spreading ruin and disaster on all sides. It was an axiom at Malvern House that if there was a chair in any room in which he happened to be, Wooster would trip over it. The child,' said Aubrey Upjohn, 'is the father of the man.'

'Frightfully sorry,' I said.

'Too late to be sorry now. A new pair of trousers ruined. It is doubtful if anything can remove the stain of tea from white flannel. Still, one must hope for the best.'

Whether I was right or wrong at this point in patting him on the shoulder and saying 'That's the spirit!' I find it difficult to decide. Wrong, probably, for it did not seem to soothe. He gave me another of those looks and strode off, smelling strongly of tea.

'Shall I tell you something, Bertie?' said Bobbie, following him with a thoughtful eye. 'That walking tour Upjohn was going to invite you to take with him is off. You will get no Christmas present from him this year, and don't expect him to come and tuck you up in bed tonight.'

I upset the milk jug with an imperious wave of the hand.

'Never mind about Upjohn and Christmas presents and walking tours. What is Pop Glossop doing here as the butler?'

'Ah! I thought you might be going to ask that. I was meaning to tell you some time.'

'Tell me now.'

'Well, it was his idea.'

I eyed her sternly. Bertram Wooster has no objection to listening to drivel, but it must not be pure babble from the padded cell, as this appeared to be.

'His idea?'

'Yes.'

'Are you asking me to believe that Sir Roderick Glossop got up one morning, gazed at himself in the mirror, thought he was looking a little pale and said to himself, "I need a change. I think I'll try being a butler for awhile"?'

'No, not that, but . . . I don't know where to begin.'

'Begin at the beginning. Come on now, young B. Wickham, smack into it,' I said, and took a piece of cake in a marked manner.

The austerity of my tone seemed to touch a nerve and kindle the fire that always slept in this vermilion-headed menace to the common weal, for she frowned a displeased frown and told me for heaven's sake to stop goggling like a dead halibut.

'I have every right to goggle like a dead halibut,' I said coldly, 'and I shall continue to do so as long as I see fit. I am under a considerable nervous s. As always seems to happen when you are mixed up in the doings, life has become one damn thing after another, and I think I am justified in demanding an explanation. I await your statement.'

'Well, let me marshal my thoughts.'

She did so, and after a brief intermission, during which I finished my piece of cake, proceeded.

'I'd better begin by telling you about Upjohn, because it all started through him. You see, he's egging Phyllis on to marry Wilbert Cream.'

'When you say egging –'

'I mean egging. And when a man like that eggs, something has to give, especially when the girl's a pill like Phyllis, who always does what Daddy tells her.'

'No will of her own?'

'Not a smidgeon. To give you an instance, a couple of days ago he took her to Birmingham to see the repertory company's performance of Chekhov's *Seagull*, because he thought it would be educational. I'd like to catch anyone trying to make me see Chekhov's *Seagull*, but Phyllis just bowed her head and said, "Yes, Daddy." Didn't even attempt to put up a fight. That'll show you how much of a will of her own she's got.'

It did indeed. Her story impressed me profoundly. I knew Chekhov's *Seagull*. My Aunt Agatha had once made me take her son Thos to a performance of it at the Old Vic, and what with the strain of trying to follow the cock-eyed goings-on of characters called Zarietchnaya and Medvienko and having to be constantly on the alert to prevent Thos making a sneak for the great open spaces, my suffering had been intense. I needed no further evidence to tell me that Phyllis Mills was a girl whose motto would always be 'Daddy knows best'. Wilbert had only got to propose and she would sign on the dotted line because Upjohn wished it.

'Your aunt's worried sick about it.'

'She doesn't approve?'

'Of course she doesn't approve. You must have heard of Willie Cream, going over to New York so much.'

'Why yes, news of his escapades has reached me. He's a playboy.'

'Your aunt thinks he's a screwball.'

'Many playboys are, I believe. Well, that being so, one can understand why she doesn't want those wedding bells to ring out. But,' I said, putting my finger on the *res* in my unerring way, 'that doesn't explain where Pop Glossop comes in.'

'Yes, it does. She got him here to observe Wilbert.'

I found myself fogged.

'Cock an eye at him, you mean? Drink him in, as it were? What good's that going to do?'

She snorted impatiently.

'Observe in the technical sense. You know how these brain specialists work. They watch the subject closely. They engage him in conversation. They apply subtle tests. And sooner or later –'

'I begin to see. Sooner or later he lets fall an incautious word to the effect that he thinks he's a poached egg, and then they've got him where they want him.'

'Well, he does something which tips them off. Your aunt was moaning to me about the situation, and I suddenly had this inspiration of bringing Glossop here. You know how I get sudden inspirations.'

'I do. That hot-water-bottle episode.'

'Yes, that was one of them.'

'Ha!'

'What did you say?'

'Just "Ha!"'

'Why "Ha!"?'

'Because when I think of that night of terror, I feel like saying "Ha!"'

She seemed to see the justice of this. Pausing merely to eat a cucumber sandwich, she proceeded.

'So I said to your aunt, "I'll tell you what to do," I said. "Get Glossop here," I said, "and have him observe Wilbert Cream. Then you'll be in a position to go to Upjohn and pull the rug from under him."'

Again I was not abreast. There had been, as far as I could recollect, no mention of any rug.

'How do you mean?'

'Well, isn't it obvious? "Rope in old Glossop," I said, "and let him observe. Then you'll be in a position," I said, "to go to Upjohn and tell him that Sir Roderick Glossop, the greatest alienist in England, is convinced that Wilbert Cream is round the bend and to ask him if he proposes to marry his stepdaughter to a man who at any moment may be marched off and added to the membership list of Colney Hatch." Even Upjohn would shrink from doing a thing like that. Or don't you think so?'

I weighed this.

'Yes,' I said, 'I should imagine you were right. Quite possibly Upjohn has human feelings, though I never noticed them when I was *in statu pupillari*, as I believe the expression is. One sees now why Glossop is at Brinkley Court. What one doesn't see is why one finds him buttling.'

'I told you that was his idea. He thought he was such a celebrated figure that it would arouse Mrs Cream's suspicions if he came here under his own name.'

'I see what you mean. She would catch him observing Wilbert and wonder why –'

'– and eventually put two and two together –'

'– and start Hey-what's-the-big-idea-ing.'

'Exactly. No mother likes to find that her hostess has got a brain specialist down to observe the son who is the apple of her eye. It hurts her feelings.'

'Whereas, if she catches the butler observing him, she merely says to herself, "Ah, an observant butler." Very sensible. With this deal Uncle Tom's got on with Homer Cream, it would be fatal to risk giving her the pip in any way. She would kick to Homer, and Homer would draw himself up and say "After what has occurred, Travers, I would prefer to break off the negotiations," and Uncle Tom would lose a packet. What is this deal they've got on, by the way? Did Aunt Dahlia tell you?'

'Yes, but it didn't penetrate. It's something to do with some land your uncle owns somewhere, and Mr Cream is thinking of buying it and putting up hotels and things. It doesn't matter, anyway. The fundamental thing, the thing to glue the eye on, is that the Cream contingent have to be kept sweetened at any cost. So not a word to a soul.'

'Quite. Bertram Wooster is not a babbler. No spiller of the beans he. But why are you so certain that Wilbert Cream is loopy? He doesn't look loopy to me.'

'Have you met him?'

'Just for a moment. He was in a leafy glade, reading poetry to the Mills girl.'

She took this big.

'Reading *poetry*? To *Phyllis*?'

'That's right. I thought it odd that a chap like him should be doing such a thing. Limericks, yes. If he had been reciting limericks to her, I could have understood it. But this was stuff from one of those books they bind in limp purple leather and sell at Christmas. I wouldn't care to swear to it, but it sounded to me extremely like Omar Khayyám.'

She continued to take it big.

'Break it up, Bertie, break it up! There's not a moment to be lost. You must go and break it up immediately.'

'Who, me? Why me?'

'That's what you're here for. Didn't your aunt tell you? She wants you to follow Wilbert Cream and Phyllis about everywhere and see that he doesn't get a chance of proposing.'

'You mean that I'm to be a sort of private eye or shamus, tailing them up? I don't like it,' I said dubiously.

'You don't have to like it,' said Bobbie. 'You just do it.'

5

Wax in the hands of the other sex, as the expression is,
I went and broke it up as directed, but not blithely.
It is never pleasant for a man of sensibility to find
himself regarded as a buttinski and a trailing arbutus,
and it was thus, I could see at a g., that Wilbert Cream
was pencilling me in. At the moment of my arrival he
had suspended the poetry reading and had taken
Phyllis's hand in his, evidently saying or about to say
something of an intimate and tender nature. Hearing my
'What ho', he turned, hurriedly released the fin and
directed at me a look very similar to the one I had
recently received from Aubrey Upjohn. He muttered
something under his breath about someone, whose name
I did not catch, apparently having been paid to haunt the
place.

'Oh, it's you again,' he said.

Well, it was, of course. No argument about that.

'Kind of at a loose end?' he said. 'Why don't you settle
down somewhere with a good book?'

I explained that I had just popped in to tell them that
tea was now being served on the main lawn, and Phyllis
squeaked a bit, as if agitated.

'Oh, dear!' she said. 'I must run. Daddy doesn't like
me to be late for tea. He says it's not respectful to my
elders.'

I could see trembling on Wilbert Cream's lips a
suggestion as to where Daddy could stick himself and
his views on respect to elders, but with a powerful effort
he held it back.

'I shall take Poppet for a walk,' he said, chirruping to

40

the dachshund, who was sniffing at my legs, filling his
lungs with the delicious Wooster bouquet.

'No tea?' I said.

'No.'

'There are muffins.'

'Tchah!' he ejaculated, if that's the word, and strode
off, followed by the low-slung dog, and it was borne in
upon me that here was another source from which I
could expect no present at Yule-Tide. His whole
demeanour made it plain that I had not added to my
little circle of friends. Though going like a breeze with
dachshunds, I had failed signally to click with Wilbert
Cream.

When Phyllis and I reached the lawn, only Bobbie was
at the tea table, and this surprised us both.

'Where's Daddy?' Phyllis asked.

'He suddenly decided to go to London,' said Bobbie.

'To London?'

'That's what he said.'

'Why?'

'He didn't tell me.'

'I must go and see him,' said Phyllis, and buzzed off.
Bobbie seemed to be musing.

'Do you know what I think, Bertie?'

'What?'

'Well, when Upjohn came out just now, he was all of a
doodah, and he had this week's *Thursday Review* in his
hand. Came by the afternoon post, I suppose. I think he
had been reading Reggie's comment on his book.'

This seemed plausible. I number several authors
among my aquaintance – the name of Boko Fittleworth
is one that springs to the mind – and they invariably
become all of a doodah when they read a stinker in the
press about their latest effort.

'Oh, you know about that thing Kipper wrote?'

'Yes, he showed it to me one day when we were
having lunch together.'

'Very mordant, I gathered from what he told me. But I don't see why that should make Upjohn bound up to London.'

'I suppose he wants to ask the editor who wrote the thing, so that he can horsewhip him on the steps of his club. But of course they won't tell him, and it wasn't signed so . . . Oh, hullo, Mrs Cream.'

The woman she was addressing was tall and thin with a hawk-like face that reminded me of Sherlock Holmes. She had an ink spot on her nose, the result of working on her novel of suspense. It is virtually impossible to write a novel of suspense without getting a certain amount of ink on the beezer. Ask Agatha Christie or anyone.

'I finished my chapter a moment ago, so I thought I would stop for a cup of tea,' said this literateuse. 'No good overdoing it.'

'No. Quit when you're ahead of the game, that's the idea. This is Mrs Travers's nephew Bertie Wooster,' said Bobbie with what I considered a far too apologetic note in her voice. If Roberta Wickham has one fault more pronounced than another, it is that she is inclined to introduce me to people as if I were something she would much have preferred to hush up. 'Bertie loves your books,' she added, quite unnecessarily, and the Cream started like a Boy Scout at the sound of a bugle.

'Oh, do you?'

'Never happier than when curled up with one of them,' I said, trusting that she wouldn't ask me which one of them I liked best.

'When I told him you were here, he was overcome.'

'Well, that certainly is great. Always glad to meet the fans. Which of my books do you like best?'

And I had got as far as 'Er' and was wondering, though not with much hope, if 'All of them' would meet the case, when Pop Glossop joined us with a telegram for Bobbie on a salver. From her mother, I presumed, calling me some name which she had forgotten to insert in previous communications. Or, of course, possibly expressing once more her conviction that I was a guffin, which, I thought, having had time to ponder over it, would be something in the nature of a bohunkus or a hammerhead.

'Oh, thank you, Swordfish,' said Bobbie, taking the 'gram.

It was fortunate that I was not holding a tea cup as she spoke, for hearing Sir Roderick thus addressed I gave another of my sudden starts and, had I had such a cup in my hand, must have strewn its contents hither and thither like a sower going forth sowing. As it was, I merely sent a cucumber sandwich flying through the air.

'Oh, sorry,' I said, for it had missed the Cream by a hair's breadth.

I could have relied on Bobbie to shove her oar in. The girl had no notion of passing a thing off.

'Excuse it, please,' she said. 'I ought to have warned you. Bertie is training for the Jerk The Cucumber Sandwich event at the next Olympic Games. He has to be practising all the time.'

On Ma Cream's brow there was a thoughtful wrinkle, as though she felt unable to accept this explanation of what had occurred. But her next words showed that it was not on my activities that her mind was dwelling but on the recent Swordfish. Having followed him with a keen glance as he faded from view, she said:

'This butler of Mrs Travers's. Do you know where she got him, Miss Wickham?'

'At the usual pet shop, I think.'

'Had he references?'

'Oh, yes. He was with Sir Roderick Glossop, the brain specialist, for years. I remember Mrs Travers saying Sir Roderick gave him a super-colossal reference. She was greatly impressed.'

Ma Cream sniffed.

'References can be forged.'

'Good gracious! Why do you say that?'

'Because I am not at all easy in my mind about this man. He has a criminal face.'

'Well, you might say that about Bertie.'

'I feel that Mrs Travers should be warned. In my *Blackness at Night* the butler turned out to be one of a gang of crooks, planted in the house to make it easy for them to break in. The inside stand, it's called. I strongly suspect that this is why this Swordfish is here, though of course it is quite possible that he is working on his own. One thing I am sure of, and that is that he is not a genuine butler.'

'What makes you think that?' I asked, handkerchiefing my upper slopes, which had become considerably bedewed. I didn't like this line of talk at all. Let the Cream get firmly in her nut the idea that Sir Roderick Glossop was not the butler, the whole butler and nothing but the butler, and disaster, as I saw it, loomed. She would probe and investigate, and before you could say 'What ho' would be in full possession of the facts. In which event, bim would go Uncle Tom's chance of scooping in a bit of easy money. And ever since I've known him failure to get his hooks on any stray cash that's floating around has always put him out of touch with the blue bird. It isn't that he's mercenary. It's just that he loves the stuff.

Her manner suggested that she was glad I had asked her that.

'I'll tell you what makes me think it. He betrays his amateurishness in a hundred ways. This very morning I found him having a long conversation with Wilbert. A real butler would never do that. He would feel it was a liberty.'

I contested this statement.

'Now there,' I said, 'I take issue with you, if taking issue means what I think it means. Many of my happiest

44

hours have been passed chatting with butlers, and it has nearly always happened that it was they who made the first advances. They seek me out and tell me about their rheumatism. Swordfish looks all right to me.'

'You are not a student of criminology, as I am. I have the trained eye, and my judgment is never wrong. That man is here for no good.'

I could see that all this was making Bobbie chafe, but her better self prevailed and she checked the heated retort. She is very fond of T. Portarlington Travers, who, she tells me, is the living image of a wire-haired terrier now residing with the morning stars but at one time very dear to her, and she remembered that for his sake the Cream had to be deferred to and handled with gloves. When she spoke, it was with the mildness of a cushat dove addressing another cushat dove from whom it was hoping to borrow money.

'But don't you think, Mrs Cream, that it may be just your imagination? You have such a wonderful imagination. Bertie was saying only the other day that he didn't know how you did it. Write all those frightfully imaginative books, I mean. Weren't you, Bertie?'

'My very words.'

'And if you have an imagination, you can't help imagining. Can you, Bertie?'

'Dashed difficult.'

Her honeyed words were wasted. The Cream continued to dig her toes in like Balaam's ass, of whom you have doubtless heard.

'I'm not imagining that that butler is up to something fishy,' she said tartly. 'And I should have thought it was pretty obvious what that something was. You seem to have forgotten that Mr Travers has one of the finest collections of old silver in England.'

This was correct. Owing possibly to some flaw in his mental make-up, Uncle Tom has been collecting old silver since I was so high, and I suppose the contents of the room on the ground floor where he parks the stuff are worth a princely sum. I knew all about that collection of his, not only because I had had to listen to him for hours on the subject of sconces, foliation, ribbon wreaths in high relief and gadroon borders, but because I had what you might call a personal interest in it, once having stolen an eighteenth-century cow-creamer for him. (Long story. No time to go into it now. You will find it elsewhere in the archives.)

'Mrs Travers was showing it to Willie the other day, and he was thrilled. Willie collects old silver himself.'

With each hour that passed I was finding it more and more difficult to get a toe-hold on the character of W. Cream. An in-and-out performer, if ever there was one. First all that poetry, I mean, and now this. I had always supposed that playboys didn't give a hoot for anything except blondes and cold bottles. It just showed once again that half the world doesn't know how the other three-quarters lives.

'He says there are any number of things in Mr Travers's collection that he would give his back teeth for. There was an eighteenth-century cow-creamer he particularly coveted. So keep your eye on that butler. I'm certainly going to keep mine. Well,' said the Cream, rising, 'I must be getting back to my work. I always like to rough out a new chapter before finishing for the day.'

She legged it, and for a moment silence reigned. Then Bobbie said, 'Phew!' and I agreed that 'Phew!' was the *mot juste*.

'We'd better get Glossop out of here quick,' I said.

'How can we? It's up to your aunt to do that, and she's away.'

'Then I'm jolly well going to get out myself. There's too much impending doom buzzing around these parts for my taste. Brinkley Court, once a peaceful country-house, has become like something sinister out of Edgar Allan Poe, and it makes my feet cold. I'm leaving.'

'You can't till your aunt gets back. There has to be some sort of host or hostess here, and I simply must go home tomorrow and see Mother. You'll have to clench your teeth and stick it.'

'And the severe mental strain to which I am being subjected doesn't matter, I suppose?'

'Not a bit. Does you good. Keeps your pores open.'

I should probably have said something pretty cutting in reply to this, if I could have thought of anything, but as I couldn't I didn't.

'What's Aunt Dahlia's address?' I said.

'Royal Hotel, Eastbourne. Why?'

'Because,' I said, taking another cucumber sandwich, 'I'm going to wire her to ring me up tomorrow without fail, so that I can apprise her of what's going on in this joint.'

6

I forget how the subject arose, but I remember Jeeves once saying that sleep knits up the ravelled sleave of care. Balm of hurt minds, he described it as. The idea being, I took it, that if things are getting sticky, they tend to seem less glutinous after you've had your eight hours.

Apple sauce, in my opinion. It seldom pans out that way with me, and it didn't now. I had retired to rest taking a dim view of the current situation at Brinkley Court and opening my eyes to a new day, as the expression is, I found myself taking an even dimmer. Who knew, I asked myself as I practically pushed the breakfast egg away untasted, what Ma Cream might not at any moment uncover? And who could say how soon, if I continued to be always at his side, Wilbert Cream would get it up his nose and start attacking me with tooth and claw? Already his manner was that of a man whom the society of Bertram Wooster had fed to the tonsils, and one more sight of the latter at his elbow might quite easily make him decide to take prompt steps through the proper channels.

Musing along these lines, I had little appetite for lunch, though Anatole had extended himself to the utmost. I winced every time the Cream shot a sharp, suspicious look at Pop Glossop as he messed about at the sideboard, and the long, loving looks her son Wilbert kept directing at Phyllis Mills chilled me to the marrow. At the conclusion of the meal he would, I presumed, invite the girl to accompany him again to that leafy glade, and it was idle to suppose that there would not be pique on his part, or even chagrin, when I came along, too.

Fortunately, as we rose from the table, Phyllis said she was going to her room to finish typing Daddy's speech, and my mind was eased for the nonce. Even a New York playboy, accustomed from his earliest years to pursue blondes like a bloodhound, would hardly follow her there and press his suit.

Seeming himself to recognize that there was nothing constructive to be done in that direction for the moment, he said in a brooding voice that he would take Poppet for a walk. This, apparently, was his invariable method of healing the stings of disappointment, and an excellent thing of course from the point of view of a dog who liked getting around and seeing the sights. They headed for the horizon and passed out of view; the hound gambolling, he not gambolling but swishing his stick a good deal in an overwrought sort of manner, and I, feeling that this was a thing that ought to be done, selected one of Ma Cream's books from Aunt Dahlia's shelves and took it out to read in a deck chair on the lawn. And I should no doubt have enjoyed it enormously, for the Cream unquestionably wielded a gifted pen, had not the warmth of the day caused me to drop off into a gentle sleep in the middle of Chapter Two.

Waking from this some little time later and running an eye over myself to see if the ravelled sleave of care had been knitted up – which it hadn't – I was told that I was wanted on the telephone. I hastened to the instrument, and Aunt Dahlia's voice came thundering over the wire.

'Bertie?'

'Bertram it is.'

'Why the devil have you been such a time? I've been hanging on to this damned receiver a long hour by Shrewsbury clock.'

'Sorry. I came on winged feet, but I was out on the lawn when you broke loose.'

'Sleeping off your lunch, I suppose?'

'My eyes may have closed for a moment.'

'Always eating, that's you.'

'It is customary, I believe, to take a little nourishment at about this hour,' I said rather stiffly. 'How's Bonzo?'

'Getting along.'

'What was it?'

'German measles, but he's out of danger. Well, what's all the excitement about? Why did you want me to phone you? Just so that you could hear Auntie's voice?'

'I am always glad to hear Auntie's voice, but I had a deeper and graver reason. I thought you ought to know about all these lurking perils in the home.'

'What lurking perils?'

'Ma Cream for one. She's hotting up. She entertains suspicions.'

'What of?'

'Pop Glossop. She doesn't like his face.'

'Well, hers is nothing to write home about.'

'She thinks he isn't a real butler.'

From the fact that my ear-drum nearly split in half I deduced that she had laughed a jovial laugh.

'Let her think.'

'You aren't perturbed?'

'Not a bit. She can't do anything about it. Anyway, Glossop ought to be leaving in about a week. He told me he didn't think it would take longer than that to make up his mind about Wilbert. Adela Cream doesn't worry me.'

'Well, if you say so, but I should have thought she was a menace.'

'She doesn't seem so to me. Anything else on your mind?'

'Yes, this Wilbert-Cream-Phyllis-Mills thing.'

'Ah, now you're talking. That's important. Did young

Bobbie Wickham tell you that you'd got to stick to
Wilbert closer than –'

'A brother?'

'I was going to say porous plaster, but have it your
own way. She explained the position of affairs?'

'She did, and it's precisely that that I want to thresh
out with you.'

'Do what out?'

'Thresh.'

'All right, start threshing.'

Having given the situation the best of the Wooster
brain for some considerable time, I had the *res* all clear
in my mind. I proceeded to decant it.

'As we go through this life, my dear old ancestor,' I
said, 'we should always strive to see the other fellow's
side of a thing, the other fellow in the case under
advisement being Wilbert Cream. Has it occurred to you
to put yourself in Wilbert Cream's place and ask yourself
how he's going to feel, being followed around all the
time? It isn't as if he was Mary.'

'What did you say?'

'I said it wasn't as if he was Mary. Mary, as I
remember, enjoyed the experience of being tailed up.'

'Bertie, you're tight.'

'Nothing of the kind.'

'Say "British constitution."'

I did so.

'And now "She sells sea shells by the sea shore."'

I reeled it off in a bell-like voice.

'Well, you seem all right,' she said grudgingly. 'How
do you mean he isn't Mary? Mary who?'

'I don't think she had a surname, had she? I was
alluding to the child who had a little lamb with fleece as
white as snow, and everywhere that Mary went the lamb
was sure to go. Now I'm not saying that I have fleece as
white as snow, but I *am* going everywhere that Wilbert
Cream goes, and one speculates with some interest as to

what the upshot will be. He resents my constant
presence.'

'Has he said so?'

'Not yet. But he gives me nasty looks.'

'That's all right. He can't intimidate me.'

I saw that she was missing the gist.

'Yes, but don't you see the peril that looms?'

'I thought you said it lurked.'

'*And* looms. What I'm driving at is that if I persist in
this porous plastering, a time must inevitably come
when, feeling that actions speak louder than words, he
will haul off and bop me one. In which event, I shall
have no alternative but to haul off and bop *him* one. The
Woosters have their pride. And when I bop them, they
stay bopped till nightfall.'

She bayed like a foghorn, showing that she was
deeply stirred.

'You'll do nothing of the sort, unless you want to have
an aunt's curse delivered on your doorstep by special
messenger. Don't you dare to start mixing it with that
man, or I'll tattoo my initials on your chest with a meat
axe. Turn the other cheek, you poor fish. If my nephew
socked her son, Adela Cream would never forgive me.
She would go running to her husband –'

' – and Uncle Tom's deal would be dished. That's the
very point I'm trying to make. If Wilbert Cream is bust
by anyone, it must be by somebody having no
connection with the Travers family. You must at once
engage a substitute for Bertram.'

'Are you suggesting that I hire a private detective?'

' "Eye" is the more usual term. No, not that, but you
must invite Kipper Herring down here. Kipper is the
man you want. He will spring to the task of dogging
Wilbert's footsteps, and if Wilbert bops him and he bops
Wilbert, it won't matter, he being outside talent. Not
that I anticipate that Wilbert will dream of doing so, for
Kipper's mere appearance commands respect. The

muscles of his brawny arms are strong as iron bands, and he has a cauliflower ear.'

There was a silence of some moments, and it was not difficult to divine that she was passing my words under review, this way and that dividing the swift mind, as I have heard Jeeves put it. When she spoke, it was in quite an awed voice.

'Do you know, Bertie, there are times – rare, yes, but they do happen – when your intelligence is almost human. You've hit it. I never thought of young Herring. Do you think he could come?'

'He was saying to me only the day before yesterday that his dearest wish was to cadge an invitation. Anatole's cooking is green in his memory.'

'Then send him a wire. You can telephone it to the post office. Sign it with my name.'

'Right-ho.'

'Tell him to drop everything and come running.'

She rang off, and I was about to draft the communication, when, as so often happens to one on relaxing from a great strain, I became conscious of an imperious desire for a little something quick. Oh, for a beaker full of the warm south, as Jeeves would have said. I pressed the bell, accordingly, and sank into a chair, and presently the door opened and a circular object with a bald head and bushy eyebrows manifested itself, giving me quite a start. I had forgotten that ringing bells at Brinkley Court under prevailing conditions must inevitably produce Sir Roderick Glossop.

It's always a bit difficult to open the conversation with a blend of brain specialist and butler, especially if your relations with him in the past have not been too chummy, and I found myself rather at a loss to know how to set the ball rolling. I yearned for that drink as the hart desireth the water-brook, but if you ask a butler to bring you a whisky-and-soda and he happens to be a brain specialist, too, he's quite apt to draw himself up and wither you with a glance. All depends on which side of him is uppermost at the moment. It was a relief when I saw that he was smiling a kindly smile and evidently welcoming this opportunity of having a quiet chat with Bertram. So long as we kept off the subject of hot-water bottles, it looked as if all would be well.

'Good afternoon, Mr Wooster. I had been hoping for a word with you in private. But perhaps Miss Wickham has already explained the circumstances? She has? Then that clears the air, and there is no danger of you incautiously revealing my identity. She impressed it upon you that Mrs Cream must have no inkling of why I am here?'

'Oh, rather. Secrecy and silence, what? If she knew you were observing her son with a view to finding out if he was foggy between the ears, there would be umbrage on her part, or even dudgeon.'

'Exactly.'

'And how's it coming along?'

'I beg your pardon?'

'The observing. Have you spotted any dippiness in the subject?'

'If by that expression you mean have I formed any definite views on Wilbert Cream's sanity, the answer is no. It is most unusual for me not to be able to make up my mind after even a single talk with the person I am observing, but in young Cream's case I remain uncertain. On the one hand, we have his record.'

'The stink bombs?'

'Exactly.'

'And the cheque-cashing with levelled gat?'

'Precisely. And a number of other things which one would say pointed to a mental unbalance. Unquestionably Wilbert Cream is eccentric.'

'But you feel the time has not yet come to measure him for the strait waistcoat?'

'I would certainly wish to observe further.'

'Jeeves told me there was something about Wilbert Cream that someone had told him when we were in New York. That might be significant.'

'Quite possibly. What was it?'

'He couldn't remember.'

'Too bad. Well, to return to what I was saying, the young man's record appears to indicate some deep-seated neurosis, if not actual schizophrenia, but against this must be set the fact that he gives no sign of this in his conversation. I was having quite a long talk with him yesterday morning, and found him most intelligent. He is interested in old silver, and spoke with a great deal of enthusiasm of an eighteenth-century cow-creamer in your uncle's collection.'

'He didn't say he *was* an eighteenth-century cow-creamer?'

'Certainly not.'

'Probably just wearing the mask.'

'I beg your pardon?'

'I mean crouching for the spring, as it were. Lulling you into security. Bound to break out sooner or later in some direction or other. Very cunning, these fellows with deep-seated neuroses.'

He shook his head reprovingly.

'We must not judge hastily, Mr Wooster. We must keep an open mind. Nothing is ever gained by not pausing to weigh the evidence. You may remember that at one time I reached a hasty judgment regarding your sanity. Those twenty-three cats in your bedroom.'

I flushed hotly. The incident had taken place several years previously, and it would have been in better taste, I considered, to have let the dead past bury its dead.

'That was explained fully.'

'Exactly. I was shown to be in error. And that is why I say I must not form an opinion prematurely in the case of Wilbert Cream. I must wait for further evidence.'

'And weigh it?'

'And, as you say, weigh it. But you rang, Mr Wooster. Is there anything I can do for you?'

'Well, as a matter of fact, I wanted a whisky-and-soda, but I hate to trouble you.'

'My dear Mr Wooster, you forget that I am, if only temporarily, a butler and, I hope, a conscientious one. I will bring it immediately.'

I was wondering, as he melted away, if I ought to tell him that Mrs Cream, too, was doing a bit of evidence-weighing, and about him, but decided on the whole better not. No sense in disturbing his peace of mind. It seemed to me that having to answer to the name of Swordfish was enough for him to have to cope with for the time being. Given too much to think about, he would fret and get pale.

When he returned, he brought with him not only the beaker full of the warm south, on which I flung myself gratefully, but a letter which he said had just come for me by the afternoon post. Having slaked the thirst, I glanced at the envelope and saw that it was from Jeeves. I opened it without much of a thrill, expecting that he would merely be informing me that he had reached his destination safely and expressing a hope that this would find me in the pink as it left him at present. In short, the usual guff.

It wasn't the usual guff by a mile and a quarter. One glance at its contents and I was Gosh-ing sharply, causing Pop Glossop to regard me with a concerned eye.

'No bad news, I trust, Mr Wooster?'

'It depends what you call bad news. It's front-page stuff, all right. This is from Jeeves, my man, now shrimping at Herne Bay, and it casts a blinding light on the private life of Wilbert Cream.'

'Indeed? This is most interesting.'

'I must begin by saying that when Jeeves was leaving for his annual vacation, the subject of W. Cream came up in the home, Aunt Dahlia having told me he was one

of the inmates here, and we discussed him at some
length. I said this, if you see what I mean, and Jeeves
said that, if you follow me. Well, just before Jeeves
pushed off, he let fall that significant remark I
mentioned just now, the one about having heard
something about Wilbert and having forgotten it. If it
came back to him, he said, he would communicate with
me. And he has, by Jove! Do you know what he says in
this missive? Give you three guesses.'

'Surely this is hardly the time for guessing games?'

'Perhaps you're right, though they're great fun, don't
you think? Well, he says that Wilbert Cream is a . . .
what's the word?' I referred to the letter. 'A
kleptomaniac,' I said. 'Which means, if the term is not
familiar to you, a chap who flits hither and thither
pinching everything he can lay his hands on.'

'Good gracious!'

'You might even go so far as "Lor' lumme!"'

'I never suspected this.'

'I told you he was wearing a mask. I suppose they took
him abroad to get him away from it all.'

'No doubt.'

'Overlooking the fact that there are just as many
things to pinch in England as in America. Does any
thought occur to you?'

'It most certainly does. I am thinking of your uncle's
collection of old silver.'

'Me, too.'

'It presents a grave temptation to the unhappy young
man.'

'I don't know that I'd call him unhappy. He probably
thoroughly enjoys lifting the stuff.'

'We must go to the collection room immediately.
There may be something missing.'

'Everything except the floor and ceiling, I expect. He
would have had difficulty in getting away with those.'

To reach the collection room was not the work of an

instant with us, for Pop Glossop was built for stability rather than speed, but we fetched up there in due course and my first emotion on giving it the once-over was one of relief, all the junk appearing to be *in statu quo*. It was only after Pop Glossop had said 'Woof!' and was starting to dry off the brow, for the going had been fast, that I spotted the hiatus.

The cow-creamer was not among those present.

7

This cow-creamer, in case you're interested, was a silver jug or pitcher or whatever you call it shaped, of all silly things, like a cow with an arching tail and a juvenile-delinquent expression on its face, a cow that looked as if it were planning, next time it was milked, to haul off and let the milkmaid have it in the lower ribs. Its back opened on a hinge and the tip of the tail touched the spine, thus giving the householder something to catch hold of when pouring. Why anyone should want such a revolting object had always been a mystery to me, it ranking high up on the list of things I would have been reluctant to be found dead in a ditch with, but apparently they liked that sort of jug in the eighteenth century and, coming down to more modern times, Uncle Tom was all for it and so, according to the evidence of the witness Glossop, was Wilbert. No accounting for tastes is the way one has to look at these things, one man's caviar being another man's major-general, as the old saw says.

However, be that as it may and whether you liked the bally thing or didn't, the point was that it had vanished, leaving not a wrack behind, and I was about to apprise Pop Glossop of this and canvass his views, when we were joined by Bobbie Wickham. She had doffed the shirt and Bermuda-shorts which she had been wearing and was now dressed for her journey home.

'Hullo, souls,' she said. 'How goes it? You look a bit hot and bothered, Bertie. What's up?'

I made no attempt to break the n. gently.

'I'll tell you what's up. You know that cow-creamer of Uncle Tom's?'

'No, I don't. What is it?'

'Sort of cream jug kind of thing, ghastly but very valuable. One would not be far out in describing it as Uncle Tom's ewe lamb. He loves it dearly.'

'Bless his heart.'

'It's all right blessing his heart, but the damn thing's gone.'

The still summer air was disturbed by a sound like beer coming out of a bottle. It was Pop Glossop gurgling. His eyes were round, his nose wiggled, and one could readily discern that this news item had come to him not as rare and refreshing fruit but more like a buffet on the base of the skull with a sock full of wet sand.

'Gone?'

'Gone.'

'Are you sure?'

I said that sure was just what I wasn't anything but.

'It is not possible that you may have overlooked it?'

'You can't overlook a thing like that.'

He re-gurgled.

'But this is terrible.'

'Might be considerably better, I agree.'

'Your uncle will be most upset.'

'He'll have kittens.'

'Kittens?'

'That's right.'

'Why kittens?'

'Why not?'

From the look on Bobbie's face, as she stood listening to our cross-talk act, I could see that the inner gist was passing over her head. Cryptic, she seemed to be registering it as.

'I don't get this,' she said. 'How do you mean it's gone?'

'It's been pinched.'

'Things don't get pinched in country-houses.'

'They do if there's a Wilbert Cream on the premises. He's a klep-whatever-it-is,' I said, and thrust Jeeves's letter on her. She perused it with an interested eye and having mastered its contents said, 'Cor chase my Aunt Fanny up a gum tree,' adding that you never knew what was going to happen next these days. There was, however, she said, a bright side.

'You'll be able now to give it as your considered opinion that the man is as loony as a coot, Sir Roderick.'

A pause ensued during which Pop Glossop appeared to be weighing this, possibly thinking back to coots he had met in the course of his professional career and trying to estimate their dippiness as compared with that of W. Cream.

'Unquestionably his metabolism is unduly susceptible to stresses resulting from the interaction of external excitations,' he said, and Bobbie patted him on the shoulder in a maternal sort of way, a thing I wouldn't have cared to do myself though our relations were, as I have indicated, more cordial than they had been at one time, and told him he had said a mouthful.

'That's how I like to hear you talk. You must tell Mrs Travers that when she gets back. It'll put her in a strong position to cope with Upjohn in this matter of Wilbert and Phyllis. With this under her belt, she'll be able to forbid the banns in no uncertain manner. "What price his metabolism?" she'll say, and Upjohn won't know which way to look. So everything's fine.'

'Everything,' I pointed out, 'except that Uncle Tom is short one ewe lamb.'

She chewed the lower lip.

'Yes, that's true. You have a point there. What steps do we take about that?'

She looked at me, and I said I didn't know, and then she looked at Pop Glossop, and he said he didn't know.

'The situation is an extremely delicate one. You concur, Mr Wooster?'

'Like billy-o.'

'Placed as he is, your uncle can hardly go to the young man and demand restitution. Mrs Travers impressed it upon me with all the emphasis at her disposal that the greatest care must be exercised to prevent Mr and Mrs Cream taking –'

'Umbrage?'

'I was about to say offence.'

'Just as good, probably. Not much in it either way.'

'And they would certainly take offence, were their son to be accused of theft.'

'It would stir them up like an egg whisk. I mean, however well they know that Wilbert is a pincher, they don't want to have it rubbed in.'

'Exactly.'

'It's one of the things the man of tact does not mention in their presence.'

'Precisely. So really I cannot see what is to be done. I am baffled.'

'So am I.'

'I'm not,' said Bobbie.

I quivered like a startled what-d'you-call-it. She had spoken with a cheery ring in her voice that told an experienced ear like mine that she was about to start something. In a matter of seconds by Shrewsbury clock, as Aunt Dahlia would have said, I could see that she was going to come out with one of those schemes or plans of hers that not only stagger humanity and turn the moon to blood but lead to some unfortunate male – who on the present occasion would, I strongly suspected, be me – getting immersed in what Shakespeare calls a sea of troubles, if it was Shakespeare. I had heard that ring in her voice before, to name but one time, at the moment when she was pressing the darning needle into my hand and telling me where I would find Sir Roderick

Glossop's hot-water bottle. Many people are of the opinion that Roberta, daughter of the late Sir Cuthbert and Lady Wickham of Skeldings Hall, Herts, ought not to be allowed at large. I string along with that school of thought.

Pop Glossop, having only a sketchy acquaintance with this female of the species and so not knowing that from childhood up her motto had been 'Anything goes', was all animation and tell-me-more.

'You have thought of some course of action that it will be feasible for us to pursue, Miss Wickham?'

'Certainly. It sticks out like a sore thumb. Do you know which Wilbert's room is?'

He said he did.

'And do you agree that if you snitch things when you're staying at a country-house, the only place you can park them in is your room?'

He said that this was no doubt so.

'Very well, then.'

He looked at her with what I have heard Jeeves call a wild surmise.

'Can you be . . . Is it possible that you are suggesting . . . ?'

'That somebody nips into Wilbert's room and hunts around? That's right. And it's obvious who the people's choice is. You're elected, Bertie.'

Well, I wasn't surprised. As I say, I had seen it coming. I don't know why it is, but whenever there's dirty work to be undertaken at the crossroads, the cry that goes round my little circle is always 'Let Wooster do it.' It never fails. But though I hadn't much hope that any words of mine would accomplish anything in the way of averting the doom, I put in a rebuttal.

'Why me?'

'It's young man's work.'

Though with a growing feeling that I was fighting in the last ditch, I continued rebutting.

'I don't see that,' I said. 'I should have thought a mature, experienced man of the world would have been far more likely to bring home the bacon than a novice like myself, who as a child was never any good at hunt-the-slipper. Stands to reason.'

'Now don't be difficult, Bertie. You'll enjoy it,' said Bobbie, though where she got that idea I was at a loss to understand. 'Try to imagine you're someone in the Secret Service on the track of the naval treaty which was stolen by a mysterious veiled woman diffusing a strange exotic scent. You'll have the time of your life. What did you say?'

'I said "Ha!" Suppose someone pops in?'

'Don't be silly. Mrs Cream is working on her book. Phyllis is in her room, typing Upjohn's speech. Wilbert's gone for a walk. Upjohn isn't here. The only character who could pop in would be the Brinkley Court ghost. If it does, give it a cold look and walk through it. That'll teach it not to come butting in where it isn't wanted, ha ha.'

'Ha ha,' trilled Pop Glossop.

I thought their mirth ill-timed and in dubious taste, and I let them see it by my manner as I strode off. For of course I did stride off. These clashings of will with the opposite sex always end with Bertram Wooster bowing to the inev. But I was not in jocund mood, and when Bobbie, speeding me on my way, called me her brave little man and said she had known all along I had it in me, I ignored the remark with a coldness which must have made itself felt.

It was a lovely afternoon, replete with blue sky, beaming sun, buzzing insects and what not, an afternoon that seemed to call to one to be out in the open with God's air playing on one's face and something cool in a glass at one's side, and here was I, just to oblige Bobbie Wickham, tooling along a corridor indoors on my way to search a comparative stranger's bedroom, this involving crawling on floors and routing under beds and probably getting covered with dust and fluff. The thought was a bitter one, and I don't suppose I have ever come closer to saying 'Faugh!' It amazed me that I could have allowed myself to be let in for a binge of this description simply because a woman wished it. Too bally chivalrous for our own good, we Woosters, and always have been.

As I reached Wilbert's door and paused outside doing a bit of screwing the courage to the sticking point, as I have heard Jeeves call it, I found the proceedings reminding me of something, and I suddenly remembered what. I was feeling just as I had felt in the old Malvern House epoch when I used to sneak down to Aubrey Upjohn's study at dead of night in quest of the biscuits he kept there in a tin on his desk, and there came back to me the memory of the occasion when, not letting a twig snap beneath my feet, I had entered his sanctum in pyjamas and a dressing-gown, to find him seated in his chair, tucking into the biscuits himself. A moment fraught with embarrassment. The What-does-this-mean-Wooster-ing that ensued and the aftermath next morning – six of the best on the old spot – had always remained on the tablets of my mind, if that's the expression I want.

Except for the tapping of a typewriter in a room along the corridor, showing that Ma Cream was hard at her self-appointed task of curdling the blood of the reading public, all was still. I stood outside the door for a space, letting 'I dare not' wait upon 'I would', as Jeeves tells me cats do in adages, then turned the handle softly, pushed – also softly – and, carrying on into the interior, found myself confronted by a girl in housemaid's costume who put a hand to her throat like somebody in a play and leaped several inches in the direction of the ceiling.

'Coo!' she said, having returned to terra firma and taken aboard a spot of breath. 'You gave me a start, sir!'

'Frightfully sorry, my dear old housemaid,' I responded

cordially. 'As a matter of fact, you gave *me* a start, making two starts in all. I'm looking for Mr Cream.'

'I'm looking for a mouse.'

This opened up an interesting line of thought.

'You feel there are mice in these parts?'

'I saw one this morning, when I was doing the room. So I brought Augustus,' she said, and indicated a large black cat who until then had escaped my notice. I recognized him as an old crony with whom I had often breakfasted, I wading into the scrambled eggs, he into the saucer of milk.

'Augustus will teach him,' she said.

Now, right from the start, as may readily be imagined, I had been wondering how this housemaid was to be removed, for of course her continued presence would render my enterprise null and void. You can't search rooms with the domestic staff standing on the sidelines, but on the other hand it was impossible for anyone with any claim to be a *preux chevalier* to take her by the slack of her garment and heave her out. For a while the thing had seemed an impasse, but this statement of hers that Augustus would teach the mouse gave me an idea.

'I doubt it,' I said. 'You're new here, aren't you?'

She conceded this, saying that she had taken office only in the previous month.

'I thought as much, or you would be aware that Augustus is a broken reed to lean on in the matter of catching mice. My own acquaintance with him is a longstanding one, and I have come to know his psychology from soup to nuts. He hasn't caught a mouse since he was a slip of a kitten. Except when eating, he does nothing but sleep. Lethargic is the word that springs to the lips. If you cast an eye on him, you will see that he's asleep now.'

'Coo! So he is.'

'It's a sort of disease. There's a scientific name for it. Trau-something. Traumatic symplegia, that's it. This cat has traumatic symplegia. In other words, putting it in simple language adapted to the lay mind, where other cats are content to get their eight hours, Augustus wants his twenty-four. If you will be ruled by me, you will abandon the whole project and take him back to the kitchen. You're simply wasting your time here.'

My eloquence was not without its effect. She said 'Coo!' again, picked up the cat, who muttered something drowsily which I couldn't follow, and went out, leaving me to carry on.

8

The first thing I noticed when at leisure to survey my surroundings was that the woman up top, carrying out her policy of leaving no stone unturned in the way of sucking up to the Cream family, had done Wilbert well where sleeping accommodation was concerned. What he had drawn when clocking in at Brinkley Court was the room known as the Blue Room, a signal honour to be accorded to a bachelor guest, amounting to being given star billing, for at Brinkley, as at most country-houses, any old nook or cranny is considered good enough for the celibate contingent. My own apartment, to take a case in point, was a sort of hermit's cell in which one would have been hard put to it to swing a cat, even a smaller one than Augustus, not of course that one often wants to do much cat-swinging. What I'm driving at is that when I blow in on Aunt Dahlia, you don't catch her saying 'Welcome to Meadowsweet Hall, my dear boy. I've put you in the Blue Room, where I am sure you will be comfortable.' I once suggested to her that I be put there, and all she said was '*You*?' and the conversation turned to other topics.

The furnishing of this Blue Room was solid and Victorian, it having been the GHQ of my Uncle Tom's late father, who liked things substantial. There was a four-poster bed, a chunky dressing-table, a massive writing table, divers chairs, pictures on the walls of fellows in cocked hats bending over females in muslin and ringlets and over at the far side a cupboard or *armoire* in which you could have hidden a dozen corpses. In short, there was so much space and so many things to shove things behind that most people, called on to find a silver cow-creamer there, would have said 'Oh, what's the use?' and thrown in the towel.

But where I had the bulge on the ordinary searcher was that I am a man of wide reading. Starting in early boyhood, long before they were called novels of suspense, I've read more mystery stories than you could shake a stick at, and they have taught me something – viz. that anybody with anything to hide invariably puts it on top of the cupboard or, if you prefer it, the *armoire*. This is what happened in *Murder at Mistleigh Manor*, *Three Dead on Tuesday*, *Excuse my Gat*, *Guess Who* and a dozen more standard works, and I saw no reason to suppose that Wilbert Cream would have deviated from routine. My first move, accordingly, was to take a chair and prop it against the *armoire*, and I had climbed on this and was preparing to subject the top to a close scrutiny, when Bobbie Wickham, entering on noiseless feet and speaking from about eighteen inches behind me, said:

'How are you getting on?'

Really, one sometimes despairs of the modern girl. You'd have thought that this Wickham would have learned at her mother's knee that the last thing a fellow in a highly nervous condition wants, when he's searching someone's room, is a disembodied voice in his immediate ear asking him how he's getting on. The upshot, I need scarcely say, was that I came down like a sack of coals. The pulse was rapid, the blood pressure high, and for awhile the Blue Room pirouetted about me like an adagio dancer.

When Reason returned to its throne, I found that Bobbie, no doubt feeling after that resounding crash that she was better elsewhere, had left me and that I was closely entangled in the chair, my position being in some respects similar to that of Kipper Herring when he got both legs wrapped round his neck in Switzerland. It seemed improbable that I would ever get loose without the aid of powerful machinery.

However, by pulling this way and pushing that, I made progress, and I'd just contrived to de-chair myself and was about to rise, when another voice spoke.

'For Pete's sake!' it said, and, looking up, I found that it was not, as I had for a moment supposed, from the lips of the Brinkley Court ghost that the words had proceeded, but from those of Mrs Homer Cream. She was looking at me, as Sir Roderick Glossop had recently looked at Bobbie, with a wild surmise, her whole air that of a woman who is not abreast. This time, I noticed, she had an ink spot on her chin.

'Mr Wooster!' she yipped.

Well, there's nothing much you can say in reply to 'Mr Wooster!' except 'Oh, hullo,' so I said it.

'You are doubtless surprised,' I was continuing, when she hogged the conversation again, asking me (a) what I was doing in her son's room and (b) what in the name of goodness I thought I was up to.

'For the love of Mike,' she added, driving her point home.

It is frequently said of Bertram Wooster that he is a man who can think on his feet, and if the necessity arises he can also use his loaf when on all fours. On the present occasion I was fortunate in having had that get-together with the housemaid and the cat Augustus, for it gave me what they call in France a *point d'appui*. Removing a portion of chair which had got entangled in my back hair, I said with a candour that became me well:

'I was looking for a mouse.'

If she had replied, 'Ah, yes, indeed. I understand now. A mouse, to be sure. Quite,' everything would have been nice and smooth, but she didn't.

'A mouse?' she said. 'What do you mean?'

Well, of course, if she didn't know what a mouse was,

there was evidently a good deal of tedious spadework before us, and one would scarcely have known where to start. It was a relief when her next words showed that that 'What do you mean?' had not been a query but more in the nature of a sort of heart-cry.

'What makes you think there is a mouse in this room?'

'The evidence points that way.'

'Have you seen it?'

'Actually, no. It's been lying what the French call *perdu.*'

'What made you come and look for it?'

'Oh, I thought I would.'

'And why were you standing on a chair?'

'Sort of just trying to get a bird's-eye view, as it were.'

'Do you often go looking for mice in other people's rooms?'

'I wouldn't say often. Just when the spirit moves me, don't you know?'

'I see. Well . . .'

When people say 'Well' to you like that, it usually means that they think you are outstaying your welcome and that the time has come to call it a day. She felt, I could see, that Woosters were not required in her son's sleeping apartment, and realizing that there might be something in this, I rose, dusted the knees of the trousers, and after a courteous word to the effect that I hoped the spine-freezer on which she was engaged was coming out well, left the presence. Happening to glance back as I reached the door, I saw her looking after me, that wild surmise still functioning on all twelve cylinders. It was plain that she considered my behaviour odd, and I'm not saying it wasn't. The behaviour of those who allow their actions to be guided by Roberta Wickham is nearly always odd.

The thing I wanted most at this juncture was to have a heart-to-heart talk with that young *femme fatale*, and after roaming hither and thither for a while I found her in my chair on the lawn, reading the Ma Cream book in which I had been engrossed when these doings had started. She greeted me with a bright smile, and said:

'Back already? Did you find it?'

With a strong effort I mastered my emotion and replied curtly but civilly that the answer was in the negative.

'No,' I said, 'I did not find it.'

'You can't have looked properly.'

Again I was compelled to pause and remind myself that an English gentleman does not slosh a sitting redhead, no matter what the provocation.

'I hadn't time to look properly. I was impeded in my movements by half-witted females sneaking up behind me and asking how I was getting on.'

'Well, I wanted to know.' A giggle escaped her. 'You did come down a wallop, didn't you? How art thou fallen from heaven, oh Lucifer, son of the morning, I said to myself. You're so terribly neurotic, Bertie. You must try to be less jumpy. What you need is a good nerve tonic. I'm sure Sir Roderick would shake you up one, if you asked him. And meanwhile?'

'How do you mean, "And meanwhile"?'

'What are your plans now?'

'I propose to hoik you out of that chair and seat myself in it and take that book, the early chapters of which I found most gripping, and start catching up with my reading and try to forget.'

'You mean you aren't going to have another bash?'

'I am not. Bertram is through. You may give this to the press, if you wish.'

'But the cow-creamer. How about your Uncle Tom's grief and agony when he learns of his bereavement?'

'Let Uncle Tom eat cake.'

'Bertie! Your manner is strange.'

'Your manner would be strange if you'd been sitting

on the floor of Wilbert Cream's sleeping apartment with a chair round your neck, and Ma Cream had come in.'

'Golly! Did she?'

'In person.'

'What did you say?'

'I said I was looking for a mouse.'

'Couldn't you think of anything better than that?'

'No.'

'And how did it all come out in the end?'

'I melted away, leaving her plainly convinced that I was off my rocker. And so, young Bobbie, when you speak of having another bash, I merely laugh bitterly,' I said, doing so. 'Catch me going into that sinister room again! Not for a million pounds sterling, cash down in small notes.'

She made what I believe, though I wouldn't swear to it, is called a *moue*. Putting the lips together and shoving them out, if you know what I mean. The impression I got was that she was disappointed in Bertram, having expected better things, and this was borne out by her next words.

'Is this the daredevil spirit of the Woosters?'

'As of even date, yes.'

'Are you man or mouse?'

'Kindly do not mention that word "mouse" in my presence.'

'I do think you might try again. Don't spoil the ship for a ha'porth of tar. I'll help you this time.'

'Ha!'

'Haven't I heard that word before somewhere?'

'You may confidently expect to hear it again.'

'No, but listen, Bertie. Nothing can possibly go wrong if we work together. Mrs Cream won't show up this time. Lightning never strikes twice in the same place.'

'Who made that rule?'

'And if she does . . . Here's what I thought we'd do.

You go in and start searching, and I'll stand outside the door.'

'You feel that will be a lot of help?'

'Of course it will. If I see her coming, I'll sing.'

'Always glad to hear you singing, of course, but in what way will that ease the strain?'

'Oh, Bertie, you really are an abysmal chump. Don't you get it? When you hear me burst into song, you'll know there's peril afoot and you'll have plenty of time to nip out of the window.'

'And break my bally neck?'

'How can you break your neck? There's a balcony outside the Blue Room. I've seen Wilbert Cream standing on it, doing his Daily Dozen. He breathes deeply and ties himself into a lovers' knot and –'

'Never mind Wilbert Cream's excesses.'

'I only put that in to make it more interesting. The point is that there is a balcony and once on it you're home. There's a water pipe at the end of it. You just slide down that and go on your way, singing a gypsy song. You aren't going to tell me that you have any objection to sliding down water pipes. Jeeves says you're always doing it.'

I mused. It was true that I had slid down quite a number of water pipes in my time. Circumstances had often so moulded themselves as to make such an action imperative. It was by that route that I had left Skeldings Hall at three in the morning after the hot-water-bottle incident. So while it would be too much, perhaps, to say that I am never happier than when sliding down water pipes, the prospect of doing so caused me little or no concern. I began to see that there was something in this plan she was mooting, if mooting is the word I want.

What tipped the scale was the thought of Uncle Tom. His love for the cow-creamer might be misguided, but you couldn't get away from the fact that he was deeply attached to the beastly thing, and one didn't like the idea of him coming back from Harrogate and saying to himself 'And now for a refreshing look at the old cow-creamer' and finding it was not in residence. It would blot the sunshine from his life, and affectionate nephews hate like the dickens to blot the sunshine from the lives of uncles. It was true that I had said 'Let Uncle Tom eat cake,' but I hadn't really meant it. I could not forget that when I was at Malvern House, Bramley-on-Sea, this relative by marriage had often sent me postal orders sometimes for as much as ten bob. He, in short, had done the square thing by me, and it was up to me to do the s.t. by him.

And so it came about that some five minutes later I stood once more outside the Blue Room with Bobbie beside me, not actually at the moment singing in the wilderness but prepared so to sing if Ma Cream, modelling her strategy on that of the Assyrian, came down like a wolf on the fold. The nervous system was a bit below par, of course, but not nearly so much so as it might have been. Knowing that Bobbie would be on sentry-go made all the difference. Any gangster will tell you that the strain and anxiety of busting a safe are greatly diminished if you've a look-out man ready at any moment to say 'Cheese it, the cops!'

Just to make sure that Wilbert hadn't returned from his hike, I knocked on the door. Nothing stirred. The coast seemed c. I mentioned this to Bobbie, and she agreed that it was as c. as a whistle.

'Now a quick run-through, to see that you have got it straight. If I sing, what do you do?'

'Nip out of the window.'

'And – ?'

'Slide down the water pipe.'

'And – ?'

'Leg it over the horizon.'

'Right. In you go and get cracking,' she said, and I went in.

The dear old room was just as I'd left it, nothing changed, and my first move, of course, was to procure another chair and give the top of the *armoire* the once-over. It was a set-back to find that the cow-creamer wasn't there. I suppose these kleptomaniacs know a thing or two and don't hide the loot in the obvious place. There was nothing to be done but start the exhaustive search elsewhere, and I proceeded to do so, keeping an ear cocked for any snatch of song. None coming, it was with something of the old debonair Wooster spirit that I looked under this and peered behind that, and I had just crawled beneath the dressing-table in pursuance of my researches, when one of those disembodied voices which were so frequent in the Blue Room spoke, causing me to give my head a nasty bump.

'For goodness' sake!' it said, and I came out like a pickled onion on the end of a fork, to find that Ma Cream was once more a pleasant visitor. She was standing there, looking down at me with a what-the-hell expression on her finely chiselled face, and I didn't blame her. Gives a woman a start, naturally, to come into her son's bedroom and observe an alien trouser-seat sticking out from under the dressing-table.

We went into our routine.

'Mr Wooster!'

'Oh, hullo.'

'It's you *again*?'

'Why, yes,' I said, for this of course was perfectly correct, and an odd sound proceeded from her, not exactly a hiccup and yet not quite not a hiccup.

'Are you still looking for that mouse?'

'That's right. I thought I saw it run under there, and I was about to deal with it regardless of its age or sex.'

'What makes you think there is a mouse here?'

'Oh, one gets these ideas.'

'Do you often hunt for mice?'

'Fairly frequently.'

An idea seemed to strike her.

'You don't think you're a cat?'

'No, I'm pretty straight on that.'

'But you pursue mice?'

'Yes.'

'Well, this is very interesting. I must consult my psychiatrist when I get back to New York. I'm sure he will tell me that this mouse-fixation is a symbol of something. Your head feels funny, doesn't it?'

'It does rather,' I said, the bump I had given it had been a juicy one, and the temples were throbbing.

'I thought as much. A sort of burning sensation, I imagine. Now you do just as I tell you. Go to your room and lie down. Relax. Try to get a little sleep. Perhaps a cup of strong tea would help. And . . . I'm trying to think of the name of that alienist I've heard people over here speak so highly of. Miss Wickham mentioned him yesterday. Bossom? Blossom? Glossop, that's it, Sir Roderick Glossop. I think you ought to consult him. A friend of mine is at his clinic now, and she says he's wonderful. Cures the most stubborn cases. Meanwhile, rest is the thing. Go and have a good rest.'

At an early point in these exchanges I had started to sidle to the door, and I now sidled through it, rather like a diffident crab on some sandy beach trying to avoid the attentions of a child with a spade. But I didn't go to my room and relax, I went in search of Bobbie, breathing fire. I wanted to take up with her the matter of that absence of the burst of melody. I mean, considering that a mere couple of bars of some popular song hit would have saved me from an experience that had turned the bones to water and whitened the hair from the neck up, I felt entitled to demand an explanation of why those bars had not emerged.

I found her outside the front door at the wheel of her car.

'Oh, hullo, Bertie,' she said, and a fish on ice couldn't have spoken more calmly. 'Have you got it?'

I ground a tooth or two and waved the arms in a passionate gesture.

'No,' I said, ignoring her query as to why I had chosen this moment to do my Swedish exercises. 'I haven't. But Ma Cream got me.'

Her eyes widened. She squeaked a bit.

'Don't tell me she caught you bending again?'

'Bending is right. I was half-way under the dressing-table. You and your singing,' I said, and I'm not sure I didn't add the word 'Forsooth!'

Her eyes widened a bit further, and she squeaked another squeak.

'Oh, Bertie, I'm sorry about that.'

'Me, too.'

'You see, I was called away to the telephone. Mother rang up. She wanted to tell me you were a nincompoop.'

'One wonders where she picks up such expressions.'

'From her literary friends, I suppose. She knows a lot of literary people.'

'Great help to the vocabulary.'

'Yes. She was delighted when I told her I was coming home. She wants to have a long talk.'

'About me, no doubt?'

'Yes, I expect your name will crop up. But I mustn't stay here chatting with you, Bertie. If I don't get started, I shan't hit the old nest till daybreak. It's a pity you made such a mess of things. Poor Mr Travers, he'll be broken-hearted. Still, into each life some rain must fall,' she said, and drove off, spraying gravel in all directions.

If Jeeves had been there, I would have turned to him and said 'Women, Jeeves!', and he would have said 'Yes, sir' or possibly 'Precisely, sir', and this would have healed the bruised spirit to a certain extent, but as he wasn't I merely laughed a bitter laugh and made for the lawn. A go at Ma Cream's goose-flesher might, I thought, do something to soothe the vibrating ganglions.

And it did. I hadn't been reading long when drowsiness stole over me, the tired eyelids closed, and in another couple of ticks I was off to dreamland, slumbering as soundly as if I had been the cat Augustus. I awoke to find that some two hours had passed, and it was while stretching the limbs that I remembered I hadn't sent that wire to Kipper Herring, inviting him to come and join the gang. I went to Aunt Dahlia's boudoir and repaired this omission, telephoning the communication to someone at the post office who would have been well advised to consult a good aurist. This done, I headed for the open spaces again, and was approaching the lawn with a view to getting on with my reading when, hearing engine noises in the background and turning to cast an eye in their direction, blow me tight if I didn't behold Kipper alighting from his car at the front door.

9

The distance from London to Brinkley Court being a hundred miles or so and not much more than two minutes having elapsed since I had sent off that telegram, the fact that he was now outside the Brinkley front door struck me as quick service. It lowered the record of the chap in the motoring sketch which Catsmeat Potter-Pirbright sometimes does at the Drones Club smoking concert where the fellow tells the other fellow he's going to drive to Glasgow and the other fellow says 'How far is that?' and the fellow says 'Three hundred miles' and the other fellow says 'How long will it take you to get there?' and the fellow says 'Oh, about half an hour, about half an hour.' The What-ho with which I greeted the back of his head as I approached was tinged, accordingly, with a certain bewilderment.

At the sound of the old familiar voice he spun around with something of the agility of a cat on hot bricks, and I saw that his dial, usually cheerful, was contorted with anguish, as if he had swallowed a bad oyster. Guessing now what was biting him, I smiled one of my subtle smiles. I would soon, I told myself, be bringing the roses back to his cheeks.

He gulped a bit, then spoke in a hollow voice, like a spirit at a séance.

'Hullo, Bertie.'

'Hullo.'

'So there you are.'

'Yes, here I am.'

'I was hoping I might run into you.'

'And now the dream's come true.'

'You see, you told me you were staying here.'

'Yes.'

'How's everything?'

'Pretty fruity.'

'Your aunt well?'

'Fine.'

'You all right?'

'More or less.'

'Capital. Long time since I was at Brinkley.'

'Yes.'

'Nothing much changed, I mean.'

'No.'

'Well, that's how it goes.'

He paused and did another splash of gulping, and I could see that we were about to come to the nub, all that had gone before having been merely what they call pour-parlers. I mean the sort of banana oil that passes between statesmen at conferences conducted in an atmosphere of the utmost cordiality before they tear their whiskers off and get down to cases.

I was right. His face working as if the first bad oyster had been followed by a second with even more spin on the ball, he said:

'I saw that thing in *The Times*, Bertie.'

I dissembled. I ought, I suppose, to have started bringing those roses back right away, but I felt it would be amusing to kid the poor fish along for a while, so I wore the mask.

'Ah, yes. In *The Times*. That thing. Quite. You saw it, did you?'

'At the club, after lunch. I couldn't believe my eyes.'

Well, I hadn't been able to believe mine, either, but I didn't mention this. I was thinking how like Bobbie it was, when planning this scheme of hers, not to have let him in on the ground floor. Slipped her mind, I suppose, or she may have kept it under her hat for some strange reason of her own. She had always been a girl who moved in a mysterious way her wonders to perform.

'And I'll tell you why I couldn't. You'll scarcely credit this, but only a couple of days ago she was engaged to *me*.'

'You don't say?'

'Yes, I jolly well do.'

'Engaged to you, eh?'

'Up to the hilt. And all the while she must have been contemplating this ghastly bit of treachery.'

'A bit thick.'

'If you can tell me anything that's thicker, I shall be glad to hear it. It just shows you what women are like. A frightful sex, Bertie. There ought to be a law. I hope to live to see the day when women are no longer allowed.'

'That would rather put a stopper on keeping the human race going, wouldn't it?'

'Well, who wants to keep the human race going?'

'I see what you mean. Yes, something in that, of course.'

He kicked petulantly at a passing beetle, frowned awhile and resumed.

'It's the cold, callous heartlessness of the thing that shocks me. Not a hint that she was proposing to return me to store. As short a while ago as last week, when we had a bite of lunch together, she was sketching out plans for the honeymoon with the greatest animation. And now this! Without a word of warning. You'd have thought that a girl who was smashing a fellow's life into hash would have dropped him a line, if only a postcard. Apparently that never occurred to her. She just let me get the news from the morning paper. I was stunned.'

'I bet you were. Did everything go black?'

'Pretty black. I took the rest of the day thinking it over, and this morning wangled leave from the office and got the car out and came down here to tell you . . .'

He paused, seeming overcome with emotion.

'Yes?'

'To tell you that, whatever we do, we mustn't let this thing break our old friendship.'

'Of course not. Damn silly idea.'

'It's such a very old friendship.'

'I don't know when I've met an older.'

'We were boys together.'

'In Eton jackets and pimples.'

'Exactly. And more like brothers than anything. I would share my last bar of almond rock with you, and you would cut me in fifty-fifty on your last bag of acid drops. When you had mumps, I caught them from you, and when I had measles, you caught them from me. Each helping each. So we must carry on regardless, just as if this had not happened.'

'Quite.'

'The same old lunches.'

'Oh, rather.'

'And golf on Saturdays and the occasional game of squash. And when you are married and settled down, I shall frequently look in on you for a cocktail.'

'Yes, do.'

'I will. Though I shall have to exercise an iron self-restraint to keep me from beaning that pie-faced little hornswoggler Mrs Bertram Wooster, *née* Wickham, with the shaker.'

'Ought you to call her a pie-faced little hornswoggler?'

'Why, can you think of something worse?' he said, with the air of one always open to suggestions. 'Do you know Thomas Otway?'

'I don't believe so. Pal of yours?'

'Seventeenth-century dramatist. Wrote *The Orphan*. In which play these words occur. "What mighty ills have not been done by Woman? Who was't betrayed the Capitol? A woman. Who lost Marc Antony the world? A woman. Who was the cause of a long ten years' war and laid at last old Troy in ashes? Woman. Deceitful, damnable, destructive Woman." Otway knew what he was talking about. He had the right slant. He couldn't have put it better if he had known Roberta Wickham personally.'

I smiled another subtle smile. I was finding all this extremely diverting.

'I don't know if it's my imagination, Kipper,' I said, 'but something gives me the impression that at moment of going to press you aren't too sold on Bobbie.'

He shrugged a shoulder.

'Oh, I wouldn't say that. Apart from wishing I could throttle the young twister with my bare hands and jump on the remains with hobnailed boots, I don't feel much about her one way or the other. She prefers you to me, and there's nothing more to be said. The great thing is that everything is all right between you and me.'

'You came all the way here just to make sure of that?' I said, moved.

'Well, there may possibly also have been an idea at the back of my mind that I might get invited to dig in at one of those dinners of Anatole's before going on to book a room at the "Bull and Bush" in Market Snodsbury. How is Anatole's cooking these days?'

'Superber than ever.'

'Continues to melt in the mouth, does it? It's two years since I bit into his products, but the taste still lingers. What an artist!'

'Ah!' I said, and would have bared my head, only I hadn't a hat on.

'Would it run to a dinner invitation, do you think?'

'My dear chap, of course. The needy are never turned from our door.'

'Splendid. And after the meal I shall propose to Phyllis Mills.'

'What!'

'Yes, I know what you're thinking. She is closely related to Aubrey Upjohn, you are saying to yourself. But surely, Bertie, she can't help that.'

'More to be pitied than censured, you think?'

'Exactly. We mustn't be narrow-minded. She is a sweet, gentle girl, unlike certain scarlet-headed Delilahs who shall be nameless, and I am very fond of her.'

'I thought you scarcely knew her.'

'Oh yes, we saw quite a bit of one another in Switzerland. We're great buddies.'

It seemed to me that the moment had come to bring the good news from Aix to Ghent, as the expression is.

'I don't know that I would propose to Phyllis Mills, Kipper. Bobbie might not like it.'

'But that's the whole idea, to show her she isn't the only onion in the stew and that if she doesn't want me, there are others who feel differently. What are you grinning about?'

As a matter of fact, I was smiling subtly, but I let it go.

'Kipper,' I said, 'I have an amazing story to relate.'

I don't know if you happen to take Old Doctor Gordon's Bile Magnesia, which when the liver is disordered gives instant relief, acting like magic and imparting an inward glow? I don't myself, my personal liver being always more or less in mid-season form, but I've seen the advertisements. They show the sufferer before and after taking, in the first case with drawn face and hollow eyes and the general look of one shortly about to hand in his dinner pail, in the second all beans and buck and what the French call *bien être*. Well, what I'm driving at is that my amazing story had exactly the same effect on Kipper as the daily dose for adults . . . He moved, he stirred, he seemed to feel the rush of life along his keel, and while I don't suppose he actually put on several pounds in weight as the tale proceeded, one got the distinct illusion that he was swelling like one of those rubber ducks which you fill with air before inserting them in the bath tub.

'Well, I'll be blowed!' he said, when I had placed the facts before him. 'Well, I'll be a son of a what not!'

'I thought you would be.'

'Bless her ingenious little heart! Not many girls would have got the grey matter working like that.'

'Very few.'

'What a helpmeet! Talk about service and co-operation. Have you any idea how the thing is working out?'

'Rather smoothly, I think. On reading the announcement in *The Times*, Wickham senior had hysterics and swooned in her tracks.'

'She doesn't like you?'

'That was the impression I got. It has been confirmed by subsequent telegrams to Bobbie in which she refers to me as a guffin and a gaby. She also considers me a nincompoop.'

'Well, that's fine. It looks as though, after you, I shall come to her like . . . it's on the tip of my tongue.'

'Rare and refreshing fruit?'

'Exactly. If you care to have a bet on it, five bob will get you ten that this scenario will end with a fade-out of Lady Wickham folding me in her arms and kissing me on the brow and saying she knows I will make her little girl happy. Gosh, Bertie, when I think that she – Bobbie, I mean, not Lady Wickham – will soon be mine and that shortly after yonder sun has set I shall be tucking into one of Anatole's dinners, I could dance a saraband. By the way, talking of dinner, do you suppose it would also run to a bed? The "Bull and Bush" is well spoken of in the *Automobile Guide*, but I'm always a bit wary of these country pubs. I'd much rather be at Brinkley Court, of which I have such happy memories. Could you swing it with your aunt?'

'She isn't here. She left to minister to her son Bonzo, who is down with German measles at his school. But she rang up this afternoon and instructed me to wire you to come and make a prolonged stay.'

'You're pulling my leg.'

'No, this is official.'

'But what made her think of me?'

'There's something she wants you to do for her.'

'She can have anything she asks, even unto half my
kingdom. What does she . . .' He paused, and a look of
alarm came into his face. 'Don't tell me she wants me to
present the prizes at Market Snodsbury Grammer
School, like Gussie?'

He was alluding to a mutual friend of ours of the
name of Gussie Fink-Nottle, who, hounded by the aged
relative into undertaking this task in the previous
summer, had got pickled to the gills and made an
outstanding exhibition of himself, setting up a mark at
which all future orators would shoot in vain.

'No, no, nothing like that. The prizes this year will be
distributed by Aubrey Upjohn.'

'That's a relief. How is he, by the way? You've met
him, of course?'

'Oh, yes, we got together. I spilled some tea on him.'

'You couldn't have done better.'

'He's grown a moustache.'

'That eases my mind. I wasn't looking forward to
seeing that bare upper lip of his. Remember how it used
to make us quail when he twitched it at us? I wonder
how he'll react when confronted with not only one
former pupil but two, and those two the very brace
that have probably haunted him in his dreams for the
last fifteen years. Might as well unleash me on him
now.'

'He isn't here.'

'You said he was.'

'Yes, he was and he will be, but he isn't. He's gone up
to London.'

'Isn't anybody here?'

'Certainly. There's Phyllis Mills –'

'Nice girl.'

' – and Mrs Homer Cream of New York City, NY, and

her son Wilbert. And that brings me to the something Aunt Dahlia wants you to do for her.'

I was pleased, as I put him hep on the Wilbert–Phyllis situation and revealed the part he was expected to play in it, to note that he showed no signs of being about to issue the presidential veto. He followed the set-up intelligently and when I had finished said that of course he would be only too willing to oblige. It wasn't much, he said, to ask of a fellow who esteemed Aunt Dahlia as highly as he did and who ever since she had lushed him up so lavishly two summers ago had been wishing there was something he could do in the way of buying back.

'Rely on me, Bertie,' he said. 'We can't have Phyllis tying herself up with a man who on the evidence would appear to be as nutty as a fruit cake. I will be about this Cream's bed and about his board, spying out all his ways. Every time he lures the poor girl into a leafy glade, I will be there, nestling behind some wild flower all ready to pop out and gum the game at the least indication that he is planning to get mushy. And now if you would show me to my room, I will have a bath and brush-up so as to be all sweet and fresh for the evening meal. Does Anatole still do those *Timbales de ris de veau toulousaine*?'

'And the *Sylphides à la crême d'écrevisses*.'

'There is none like him, none,' said Kipper, moistening the lips with the tip of the tongue and looking like a wolf that has just spotted its Russian peasant. 'He stands alone.'

As I hadn't the remotest which rooms were available
and which weren't, getting Kipper dug in necessitated
ringing for Pop Glossop. I pressed the button and he
appeared, giving me, as he entered, the sort of
conspiratorial glance the acting secretary of a secret
society would have given a friend on the membership
roll.

'Oh, Swordfish,' I said, having given him a
conspiratorial glance in return, for one always likes to do
the civil thing, 'this is Mr Herring, who has come to join
our little group.'

He bowed from the waist, not that he had much waist.

'Good evening, sir.'

'He will be staying some time. Where do we park
him?'

'The Red Room suggests itself, sir.'

'You get the Red Room, Kipper.'

'Right-ho.'

'I had it last year. 'Tis not as deep as a well nor as
wide as a church door, but 'tis enough, 'twill serve,' I
said, recalling a gag of Jeeves's. 'Will you escort Mr
Herring thither, Swordfish?'

'Very good, sir.'

'And when you have got him installed, perhaps I could
have a word with you in your pantry,' I said, giving him
a conspiratorial glance.

'Certainly, sir,' he responded, giving me a
conspiratorial glance.

It was one of those big evenings for conspiratorial
glances.

I hadn't been waiting in the pantry long when he navigated over the threshold, and my first act was to congratulate him on the excellence of his technique. I had been much impressed by all that 'Very good, sir,' 'Certainly, sir,' bowing-from-the-waist stuff. I said that Jeeves himself couldn't have read his lines better, and he simpered modestly and said that one picked up these little tricks of the trade from one's own butler.

'Oh, by the way,' I said, 'where did you get the Swordfish?'

He smiled indulgently.

'That was Miss Wickham's suggestion.'

'I thought as much.'

'She informed me that she had always dreamed of one day meeting a butler called Swordfish. A charming young lady. Full of fun.'

'It may be fun for her,' I said with one of my bitter laughs, 'but it isn't so diverting for the unfortunate toads beneath the harrow whom she plunges so ruthlessly in the soup. Let me tell you what occurred after I left you this afternoon.'

'Yes, I am all eagerness to hear.'

'Then pin your ears back and drink it in.'

If I do say so, I told my story well, omitting no detail however slight. It had him Bless-my-soul-ing throughout, and when I had finished he t'ck-t'ck-t'ck-ed and said it must have been most unpleasant for me, and I said that 'unpleasant' covered the facts like the skin on a sausage.

'But I think that in your place I should have thought of an explanation of your presence calculated to carry more immediate conviction than that you were searching for a mouse.'

'Such as?'

'It is hard to say on the spur of the moment.'

'Well, it was on the spur of the m. that I had to say it,' I rejoined with some heat. 'You don't get time to polish

your dialogue and iron out the bugs in the plot when a
woman who looks like Sherlock Holmes catches you in
her son's room with your rear elevation sticking out
from under the dressing-table.'

'True. Quite true. But I wonder . . .'

'Wonder what?'

'I do not wish to hurt your feelings.'

'Go ahead. My feelings have been hurt so much
already that a little bit extra won't make any difference.'

'I may speak frankly?'

'Do.'

'Well, then, I am wondering if it was altogether wise
to entrust this very delicate operation to a young fellow
like yourself. I am coming round to the view you put
forward when we were discussing the matter with Miss
Wickham. You said, if you recall, that the enterprise
should have been placed in the hands of a mature,
experienced man of the world and not in those of one of
less ripe years who as a child had never been expert at
hunt-the-slipper. I am, you will agree, mature, and in my
earlier days I won no little praise for my skill at
hunt-the-slipper. I remember one of the hostesses whose
Christmas parties I attended comparing me to a juvenile
bloodhound. An extravagant encomium, of course, but
that is what she said.'

I looked at him with a wild surmise. It seemed to me
that there was but one meaning to be attached to his
words.

'You aren't thinking of having a pop at it yourself?'

'That is precisely my intention, Mr Wooster.'

'Lord love a duck!'

'The expression is new to me, but I gather from it that
you consider my conduct eccentric.'

'Oh, I wouldn't say that, but do you realize what you
are letting yourself in for? You won't enjoy meeting Ma
Cream. She has an eye like . . . what are those things
that have eyes? Basilisks, that's the name I was groping

for. She has an eye like a basilisk. Have you considered the possibility of having that eye go through you like a dose of salts?'

'Yes, I can envisage the peril. But the fact is, Mr Wooster, I regard what has happened as a challenge. My blood is up.'

'Mine froze.'

'And you may possibly not believe me, but I find the prospect of searching Mr Cream's room quite enjoyable.'

'Enjoyable?'

'Yes. In a curious way it restores my youth. It brings back to me my preparatory school days, when I would often steal down at night to the headmaster's study to eat his biscuits.'

I started. I looked at him with a kindling eye. Deep had called to deep, and the cockles of the heart were warmed.

'Biscuits?'

'He kept them in a tin on his desk.'

'You really used to do that at your prep school?'

'Many years ago.'

'So did I,' I said, coming within an ace of saying, 'My brother!'

He raised his bushy eyebrows, and you could see that his heart's cockles were warmed, too.

'Indeed? Fancy that! I had supposed the idea original with myself, but no doubt all over England today the rising generation is doing the same thing. So you too have lived in Arcady? What kind of biscuits were yours? Mine were mixed.'

'The ones with pink and white sugar on?'

'In many instances, though some were plain.'

'Mine were ginger nuts.'

'Those are very good, too, of course, but I prefer the mixed.'

'So do I. But you had to take what you could get in those days. Were you ever copped?'

'I am glad to say never.'

'I was once. I can feel the place in frosty weather still.'

'Too bad. But these things will happen. Embarking on the present venture, I have the sustaining thought that if the worst occurs and I am apprehended, I can scarcely be given six of the best bending over a chair, as we used to call it. Yes, you may leave this little matter entirely to me, Mr Wooster.'

'I wish you'd call me Bertie.'

'Certainly, certainly.'

'And might I call you Roderick?'

'I shall be delighted.'

'Or Roddy? Roderick's rather a mouthful.'

'Whichever you prefer.'

'And you are really going to hunt the slipper?'

'I am resolved to do so. I have the greatest respect and affection for your uncle and appreciate how deeply wounded he would be, were this prized object to be permanently missing from his collection. I would never forgive myself if in the endeavour to recover his property, I were to leave any –'

'Stone unturned?'

'I was about to say avenue unexplored. I shall strain every –'

'Sinew?'

'I was thinking of the word nerve.'

'Just as *juste*. You'll have to bide your time, of course.'

'Quite.'

'And await your opportunity.'

'Exactly.'

'Opportunity knocks but once.'

'So I understand.'

'I'll give you one tip. The thing isn't on top of the cupboard or *armoire*.'

'Ah, that is helpful.'

'Unless of course he's put it there since. Well, anyway, best of luck, Roddy.'

'Thank you, Bertie.'

If I had been taking Old Doctor Gordon's Bile Magnesia regularly, I couldn't have felt more of an inward glow as I left him and headed for the lawn to get the Ma Cream book and return it to its place on the shelves of Aunt Dahlia's boudoir. I was lost in admiration of Roddy's manly spirit. He was well stricken in years, fifty if a day, and it thrilled me to think that there was so much life in the old dog still. It just showed . . . well, I don't know what, but something. I found myself musing on the boy Glossop, wondering what he had been like in his biscuit-snitching days. But except that I knew he wouldn't have been bald then, I couldn't picture him. It's often this way when one contemplates one's seniors. I remember how amazed I was to learn that my Uncle Percy, a tough old egg with apparently not a spark of humanity in him, had once held the metropolitan record for being chucked out of Covent Garden Balls.

I got the book, and ascertaining after reaching Aunt Dahlia's lair that there remained some twenty minutes before it would be necessary to start getting ready for the evening meal I took a seat and resumed my reading. I had had to leave off at a point where Ma Cream had just begun to spit on her hands and start filling the customers with pity and terror. But I hadn't put more than a couple of clues and a mere sprinkling of human gore under my belt, when the door flew open and Kipper appeared. And as the eye rested on him, he too filled me with pity and terror, for his map was flushed and his manner distraught. He looked like Jack Dempsey at the conclusion of his first conference with Gene Tunney, the occasion, if you remember, when he forgot to duck.

He lost no time in bursting into speech.

'Bertie! I've been hunting for you all over the place!'

'I was having a chat with Swordfish in his pantry. Something wrong?'

'Something wrong!'

'Don't you like the Red Room?'

'The Red Room!'

I gathered from his manner that he had not come to beef about his sleeping accommodation.

'Then what is your little trouble?'

'My little trouble!'

I felt that this sort of thing must be stopped at its source. It was only ten minutes to dressing-for-dinner time, and we could go on along these lines for hours.

'Listen, old crumpet,' I said patiently. 'Make up your mind whether you are my old friend Reginald Herring or an echo in the Swiss mountains. If you're simply going to repeat every word I say –'

At this moment Pop Glossop entered with the cocktails, and we cheesed the give-and-take. Kipper drained his glass to the lees and seemed to become calmer. When the door closed behind Roddy and he was at liberty to speak, he did so quite coherently. Taking another beaker, he said:

'Bertie, the most frightful thing has happened.'

I don't mind saying that the heart did a bit of sinking. In an earlier conversation with Bobbie Wickham it will be recalled that I had compared Brinkley Court to one of those joints the late Edgar Allan Poe used to write about. If you are acquainted with his works, you will remember that in them it was always tough going for those who stayed in country-houses, the visitor being likely at any moment to encounter a walking corpse in a winding sheet with blood all over it. Prevailing conditions at Brinkley were not perhaps quite as testing as that, but the atmosphere had undeniably become sinister, and here was Kipper more than hinting that he had a story to relate which would deepen the general feeling that things were hotting up.

'What's the matter?' I said.

'I'll tell you what's the matter,' he said.

'Yes, do,' I said, and he did.

'Bertie,' he said, taking a third one. 'I think you will understand that when I read that announcement in *The Times* I was utterly bowled over?'

'Oh quite. Perfectly natural.'

'My head swam, and –'

'Yes, you told me. Everything went black.'

'I wish it had stayed black,' he said bitterly, 'but it didn't. After awhile the mists cleared, and I sat there seething with fury. And after I had seethed for a bit I rose from my chair, took pen in hand and wrote Bobbie a stinker.'

'Oh, gosh!'

'I put my whole soul into it.'

'Oh, golly!'

'I accused her in set terms of giving me the heave-ho in order that she could mercenarily marry a richer man. I called her a carrot-topped Jezebel whom I was thankful to have got out of my hair. I . . . Oh, I can't remember what else I said but, as I say, it was a stinker.'

'But you never mentioned a word about this when I met you.'

'In the ecstasy of learning that that *Times* thing was just a ruse and that she loved me still it passed completely from my mind. When it suddenly came back to me just now, it was like getting hit in the eye with a wet fish. I reeled.'

'Squealed?'

'Reeled. I felt absolutely boneless. But I had enough strength to stagger to the telephone. I rang up Skeldings Hall and was informed that she had just arrived.'

'She must have driven like an inebriated racing motorist.'

'No doubt she did. Girls will be girls. Anyway, she was there. She told me with a merry lilt in her voice that she had found a letter from me on the hall table and could hardly wait to open it. In a shaking voice I told her not to.'

'So you were in time.'

'In time, my foot! Bertie, you're a man of the world.
You've known a good many members of the other sex in
your day. What does a girl do when she is told not to
open a letter?'

I got his drift.

'Opens it?'

'Exactly. I heard the envelope rip, and the next
moment . . . No, I'd rather not think of it.'

'She took umbrage?'

'Yes, and she also took my head off. I don't know if
you have ever been in a typhoon on the Indian Ocean.'

'No, I've never visited those parts.'

'Nor have I, but from what people tell me what
ensued must have been very like being in one. She spoke
for perhaps five minutes –'

'By Shrewsbury clock.'

'What?'

'Nothing. What did she say?'

'I can't repeat it all, and wouldn't if I could.'

'And what did you say?'

'I couldn't get a word in edgeways.'

'One can't sometimes.'

'Women talk so damn quick.'

'How well I know it! And what was the final score?'

'She said she was thankful that I was glad to have got
her out of my hair, because she was immensely relieved
to have got me out of hers, and that I had made her very
happy because now she was free to marry you, which
had always been her dearest wish.'

In this hair-raiser of Ma Cream's which I had been
perusing there was a chap of the name of Scarface
McColl, a gangster of sorts, who, climbing into the old
car one morning and twiddling the starting key, went up
in fragments owing to a business competitor having
inserted a bomb in his engine, and I had speculated for a
moment, while reading, as to how he must have felt. I

knew now. Just as he had done, I rose. I sprang to the door, and Kipper raised an eyebrow.

'Am I boring you?' he said rather stiffly.

'No, no. But I must go and get my car.'

'You going for a ride?'

'Yes.'

'But it's nearly dinner-time.'

'I don't want any dinner.'

'Where are you going?'

'Herne Bay.'

'Why Herne Bay?'

'Because Jeeves is there, and this thing must be placed in his hands without a moment's delay.'

'What can Jeeves do?'

'That,' I said, 'I cannot say, but he will do something. If he has been eating plenty of fish, as no doubt he would at a seashore resort, his brain will be at the top of its form, and when Jeeves's brain is at the top of its form, all you have to do is press a button and stand out of the way while he takes charge.'

11

It's considerably more than a step from Brinkley Court
to Herne Bay, the one being in the middle of
Worcestershire and the other on the coast of Kent, and
even under the best of conditions you don't expect to do
the trip in a flash. On the present occasion, held up by
the Arab steed getting taken with a fit of the vapours
and having to be towed to a garage for medical
treatment, I didn't fetch up at journey's end till well past
midnight. And when I rolled round to Jeeves's address on
the morrow, I was informed that he had gone out early
and they didn't know when he would be back. Leaving
word for him to ring me at the Drones, I returned to the
metropolis and was having the pre-dinner keg of nails in
the smoking-room when his call came through.

'Mr Wooster? Good evening, sir. This is Jeeves.'

'And not a moment too soon,' I said, speaking with
the emotion of a lost lamb which after long separation
from the parent sheep finally manages to spot it across
the meadow. 'Where have you been all this time?'

'I had an appointment to lunch with a friend at
Folkestone, sir, and while there was persuaded to extend
my visit in order to judge a seaside bathing belles
contest.'

'No, really? You do live, don't you?'

'Yes, sir.'

'How did it go off?'

'Quite satisfactorily, sir, thank you.'

'Who won?'

'A Miss Marlene Higgins of Brixton, sir, with Miss
Lana Brown of Tulse Hill and Miss Marilyn Bunting of

Penge honourably mentioned. All most attractive young ladies.'

'Shapely?'

'Extremely so.'

'Well, let me tell you, Jeeves, and you can paste this in your hat, shapeliness isn't everything in this world. In fact, it sometimes seems to me that the more curved and lissome the members of the opposite sex, the more likely they are to set Hell's foundations quivering. I'm sorely beset, Jeeves. Do you recall telling me once about someone who told somebody he could tell him something which would make him think a bit? Knitted socks and porcupines entered into it, I remember.'

'I think you may be referring to the ghost of the father of Hamlet, Prince of Denmark, sir. Addressing his son, he said "I could a tale unfold whose lightest word would harrow up thy soul, freeze thy young blood, make thy two eyes, like stars, start from their spheres, thy knotted and combined locks to part and each particular hair to stand on end like quills upon the fretful porpentine."'

'That's right. Locks, of course, not socks. Odd that he should have said porpentine when he meant porcupine. Slip of the tongue, no doubt, as so often happens with ghosts. Well, he had nothing on me, Jeeves. It's a tale of that precise nature that I am about to unfold. Are you listening?'

'Yes, sir.'

'Then hold on to your hat and don't miss a word.'

When I had finished unfolding, he said, 'I can readily appreciate your concern, sir. The situation, as you say, is one fraught with anxiety,' which is pitching it strong for Jeeves, he as a rule coming through with a mere 'Most disturbing, sir.'

'I will come to Brinkley Court immediately, sir.'

'Will you really? I hate to interrupt your holiday.'

'Not at all, sir.'

'You can resume it later.'

'Certainly, sir, if that is convenient to you.'

'But now –'

'Precisely sir. Now, if I may borrow a familiar phrase –'

' – is the time for all good men to come to the aid of the party?'

'The very words I was about to employ, sir. I will call at the apartment at as early an hour tomorrow as is possible.'

'And we'll drive down together. Right,' I said, and went off to my simple but wholesome dinner.

It was with . . . well, not quite an uplifted heart . . . call it a heart lifted about half way . . . that I started out for Brinkley on the following afternoon. The thought that Jeeves was at my side, his fish-fed brain at my disposal, caused a spot of silver lining to gleam through the storm clouds, but only a spot, for I was asking myself if even Jeeves might not fail to find a solution of the problem that had raised its ugly head. Admittedly expert though he was at joining sundered hearts, he had rarely been up against a rift within the lute so complete as that within the lute of Roberta Wickham and Reginald Herring, and as I remember hearing him say once, 'tis not in mortals to command success. And at the thought of what would ensue, were he to fall down on the assignment, I quivered like something in aspic. I could not forget that Bobbie, while handing Kipper his hat, had expressed in set terms her intention of lugging me to the altar rails and signalling to the clergyman to do his stuff. So as I drove along the heart, as I have indicated, was uplifted only to a medium extent.

When we were out of the London traffic and it was possible to converse without bumping into buses and pedestrians, I threw the meeting open for debate.

'You have not forgotten our telephone conversation of yestreen, Jeeves?'

'No, sir.'

'You have the salient points docketed in your mind?'

'Yes, sir.'

'Have you been brooding on them?'

'Yes, sir.'

'Got a bite of any sort?'

'Not yet, sir.'

'No, I hardly expected you would. These things always take time.'

'Yes, sir.'

'The core of the matter is,' I said, twiddling the wheel to avoid a passing hen, 'that in Roberta Wickham we are dealing with a girl of high and haughty spirit.'

'Yes, sir.'

'And girls of high and haughty spirit need kidding along. This cannot be done by calling them carrot-topped Jezebels.'

'No, sir.'

'I know if anyone called me a carrot-topped Jezebel, umbrage is the first thing I'd take. Who was Jezebel, by the way? The name seems familiar, but I can't place her.'

'A character in the Old Testament, sir. A queen of Israel.'

'Of course, yes. Be forgetting my own name next. Eaten by dogs, wasn't she?'

'Yes, sir.'

'Can't have been pleasant for her.'

'No, sir.'

'Still, that's the way the ball rolls. Talking of being eaten by dogs, there's a dachshund at Brinkley who when you first meet him will give you the impression that he plans to convert you into a light snack between his regular meals. Pay no attention. It's all eyewash. His belligerent attitude is simply –'

'Sound and fury signifying nothing, sir?'

'That's it. Pure swank. A few civil words, and he will be grappling you . . . what's that expression I've heard you use?'

'Grappling me to his soul with hoops of steel, sir?'

'In the first two minutes. He wouldn't hurt a fly, but he has to put up a front because his name's Poppet. One can readily appreciate that when a dog hears himself addressed day in and day out as Poppet, he feels he must throw his weight about. His self-respect demands it.'

'Precisely, sir.'

'You'll like Poppet. Nice dog. Wears his ears inside out. Why do dachshunds wear their ears inside out?'

'I could not say, sir.'

'Nor me. I've often wondered. But this won't do, Jeeves. Here we are, yakking about Jezebels and dachshunds, when we ought to be concentrating our minds on . . .'

I broke off abruptly. My eye had been caught by a wayside inn. Well, not actually so much by the wayside inn as by what was standing outside it – to wit, a scarlet roadster which I recognized instantly as the property of Bobbie Wickham. One saw what had happened. Driving back to Brinkley after a couple of nights with Mother, she had found the going a bit warm and had stopped off at this hostelry for a quick one. And a very sensible thing to do, too. Nothing picks one up more than a spot of sluicing on a hot summer afternoon.

I applied the brakes.

'Mind waiting here a minute, Jeeves?'

'Certainly, sir. You wish to speak to Miss Wickham?'

'Ah, you spotted her car?'

'Yes, sir. It is distinctly individual.'

'Like its owner. I have a feeling that I may be able to accomplish something in the breach-healing way with a honeyed word or two. Worth trying, don't you think?'

'Unquestionably, sir.'

'At a time like this one doesn't want to leave any avenue unturned.'

The interior of the wayside inn – the 'Fox and Goose',

not that it matters – was like the interiors of all wayside inns, dark and cool and smelling of beer, cheese, coffee, pickles and the sturdy English peasantry. Entering, you found yourself in a cosy nook with tankards on the walls and chairs and tables dotted hither and thither. On one of the chairs at one of the tables Bobbie was seated with a glass and a bottle of ginger ale before her.

'Good Lord, Bertie!' she said as I stepped up and what-ho-ed. 'Where did you spring from?'

I explained that I was on my way back to Brinkley from London in my car.

'Be careful someone doesn't pinch it. I'll bet you haven't taken out the keys.'

'No, but Jeeves is there, keeping watch and ward, as you might say.'

'Oh, you've brought Jeeves with you? I thought he was on his holiday.'

'He very decently cancelled it.'

'Pretty feudal.'

'Very. When I told him I needed him at my side, he didn't hesitate.'

'What do you need him at your side for?'

The moment had come for the honeyed word. I lowered my voice to a confidential murmur, but on her inquiring if I had laryngitis raised it again.

'I had an idea that he might be able to do something.'

'What about?'

'About you and Kipper,' I said, and started to feel my way cautiously towards the core and centre. It would be necessary, I knew, to pick my words with c., for with girls of high and haughty spirit you have to watch your step, especially if they have red hair, like Bobbie. If they think you're talking out of turn, dudgeon ensues, and dudgeon might easily lead her to reach for the ginger ale bottle and bean me with it. I don't say she would, but it was a possibility that had to be taken into account. So I sort of eased into the agenda.

'I must begin by saying that Kipper has given me a full eyewitness's – well, earwitness's I suppose you'd say – report of that chat you and he had over the telephone, and no doubt you are saying to yourself that it would have been in better taste for him to have kept it under his hat. But you must remember that we were boys together, and a fellow naturally confides in a chap he was boys together with. Anyway, be that as it may, he poured out his soul to me, and he hadn't been pouring long before I was able to see that he was cut to the quick. His blood pressure was high, his eye rolled in what they call a fine frenzy, and he was death-where-is-thy-sting-ing like nobody's business.'

I saw her quiver and kept a wary eye on the ginger ale bottle. But even if she had raised it and brought it down on the Wooster bean, I couldn't have been more stunned than I was by the words that left her lips.

'The poor lamb!'

I had ordered a gin and tonic. I now spilled a portion of this.

'Did you say poor lamb?'

'You bet I said poor lamb, though "Poor sap" would perhaps be a better description. Just imagine him taking all that stuff I said seriously. He ought to have known I didn't mean it.'

I groped for the gist.

'You were just making conversation?'

'Well, blowing off steam. For heaven's sake, isn't a girl allowed to blow off some steam occasionally? I never dreamed it would really upset him. Reggie always takes everything so literally.'

'Then is the position that the laughing love god is once more working at the old stand?'

'Like a beaver.'

'In fact, to coin a phrase, you're sweethearts still?'

'Of course. I may have meant what I said at the time, but only for about five minutes.'

I drew a deep breath, and a moment later wished I hadn't, because I drew it while drinking the remains of my gin and tonic.

'Does Kipper know of this?' I said, when I had finished coughing.

'Not yet. I'm on my way to tell him.'

I raised a point on which I particularly desired assurance.

'Then what it boils down to is – No wedding bells for me?'

'I'm afraid not.'

'Quite all right. Anything that suits you.'

'I don't want to get jugged for bigamy.'

'No, one sees that. And your selection for the day is Kipper. I don't blame you. The ideal mate.'

'Just the way I look at it. He's terrific, isn't he?'

'Colossal.'

'I wouldn't marry anyone else if they came to me bringing apes, ivory and peacocks. Tell me what he was like as a boy.'

'Oh, much the same as the rest of us.'

'Nonsense!'

'Except, of course, for rescuing people from burning buildings and saving blue-eyed children from getting squashed by runaway horses.'

'He did that a lot?'

'Almost daily.'

'Was he the Pride of the School?'

'Oh, rather.'

'Not that it was much of a school to be the pride of, from what he tells me. A sort of Dotheboys Hall, wasn't it?'

'Conditions under Aubrey Upjohn were fairly tough. One's mind reverts particularly to the sausages on Sunday.'

'Reggie was very funny about those. He said they were made not from contented pigs but from pigs which had expired, regretted by all, of glanders, the botts and tuberculosis.'

'Yes, that would be quite a fair description of them, I suppose. You going?' I said, for she had risen.

'I can't wait for another minute. I want to fling myself into Reggie's arms. If I don't see him soon, I shall pass out.'

'I know how you feel. The chap in the Yeoman's Wedding Song thought along those same lines, only the way he put it was "Ding dong, ding dong, ding dong, I hurry along". At one time I often used to render the number at village concerts, and there was a nasty Becher's Brook to get over when you got to "For it is my wedding morning," because you had to stretch out the "mor" for about ten minutes, which tested the lung power severely. I remember the vicar once telling me –'

Here I was interrupted, as I'm so often interrupted when giving my views on the Yeoman's Wedding Song, by her saying that she was dying to hear all about it but would rather wait till she could get it in my autobiography. We went out together, and I saw her off and returned to where Jeeves kept his vigil in the car, all smiles. I was all smiles, I mean, not Jeeves. The best he ever does is to let his mouth twitch slightly on one side, generally the left. I was in rare fettle, and the heart had touched a new high. I don't know anything that braces one up like finding you haven't got to get married after all.

'Sorry to keep you waiting, Jeeves,' I said. 'Hope you weren't bored?'

'Oh no, sir, thank you. I was quite happy with my Spinoza.'

'Eh?'

'The copy of Spinoza's *Ethics* which you kindly gave me some time ago.'

'Oh, ah, yes, I remember. Good stuff?'

'Extremely, sir.'

'I suppose it turns out in the end that the butler did it. Well, Jeeves, you'll be glad to hear that everything's under control.'

'Indeed, sir?'

'Yes, rift in lute mended and wedding bells liable to ring out at any moment. She's changed her mind.'

'*Varium et mutabile semper femina*, sir.'

'I shouldn't wonder. And now,' I said, climbing in and taking the wheel, 'I'll unfold the tale of Wilbert and the cow-creamer, and if that doesn't make your knotted locks do a bit of starting from their spheres, I for one shall be greatly surprised.'

12

Arriving at Brinkley in the quiet evenfall and putting the old machine away in the garage, I noticed that Aunt Dahlia's car was there and gathered from this that the aged relative was around and about once more. Nor was I in error. I found her in her boudoir getting outside a dish of tea and a crumpet. She greeted me with one of those piercing view-halloos which she had picked up on the hunting field in the days when she had been an energetic chivvier of the British fox. It sounded like a gas explosion and went through me from stem to stern. I've never hunted myself, but I understand that half the battle is being able to make noises like some jungle animal with dyspepsia, and I believe that Aunt Dahlia in her prime could lift fellow-members of the Quorn and Pytchley out of their saddles with a single yip, though separated from them by two ploughed fields and a spinney.

'Hullo, ugly,' she said. 'Turned up again, have you?'

'Just this moment breasted the tape.'

'Been to Herne Bay, young Herring tells me.'

'Yes, to fetch Jeeves. How's Bonzo?'

'Spotty but cheerful. What did you want Jeeves for?'

'Well, as it turns out, his presence isn't needed, but I only discovered that when I was half-way here. I was bringing him along to meditate . . . no, it isn't meditate . . . to mediate, that's the word, between Bobbie Wickham and Kipper. You knew they were betrothed?'

'Yes, she told me.'

'Did she tell you about shoving that thing in *The Times* saying she was engaged to me?'

'I was the first in whom she confided. I got a good laugh out of that.'

'More than Kipper did, because it hadn't occurred to the cloth-headed young nitwit to confide in him. When he read the announcement, he reeled and everything went black. It knocked his faith in woman for a loop, and after seething for a while he sat down and wrote her a letter in the Thomas Otway vein.'

'In the who's vein?'

'You are not familiar with Thomas Otway? Seventeenth-century dramatist, celebrated for making bitter cracks about the other sex. Wrote a play called *The Orphan*, which is full of them.'

'So you do read something beside the comics?'

'Well, actually I haven't steeped myself to any great extent in Thos's output, but Kipper told me about him. He held the view that women are a mess, and Kipper passed this information on to Bobbie in this letter of which I speak. It was a snorter.'

'And you never thought of explaining to him, I suppose?'

'Of course I did. But by that time she'd got the letter.'

'Why didn't the idiot tell her not to open it?'

'It was his first move. "I've found a letter from you here, precious," she said. "On no account open it, angel," he said. So of course she opened it.'

She pursed the lips, nodded the loaf, and ate a moody piece of crumpet.

'So that's why he's been going about looking like a dead fish. I suppose Roberta broke the engagement?'

'In a speech lasting five minutes without a pause for breath.'

'And you brought Jeeves along to mediate?'

'That was the idea.'

'But if things have gone as far as that . . .'

'You doubt whether even Jeeves can heal the rift?' I patted her on the top knot. 'Dry the starting tear, old ancestor, it's healed. I met her at a pub on the way here, and she told me that almost immediately after she had flipped her lid in the manner described she had a change of heart. She loves him still with a passion that's more like boiling oil than anything, and when we parted she was tooling off to tell him so. By this time they must be like ham and eggs again. It's a great burden off my mind, because, having parted brass rags with Kipper, she announced her intention of marrying me.'

'A bit of luck for you, I should have thought.'

'Far from it.'

'Why? You were crazy about the girl once.'

'But no longer. The fever has passed, the scales have fallen from my eyes, and we're just good friends. The snag in this business of falling in love, aged relative, is that the parties of the first part so often get mixed up with the wrong parties of the second part, robbed of their cooler judgment by the parties of the second part's glamour. Put it like this. The male sex is divided into rabbits and non-rabbits and the female sex into dashers and dormice, and the trouble is that the male rabbit has a way of getting attracted by the female dasher (who would be fine for the male non-rabbit) and realizing too late that he ought to have been concentrating on some mild, gentle dormouse with whom he could settle down peacefully and nibble lettuce.'

'The whole thing, in short, a bit of a mix-up?'

'Exactly. Take me and Bobbie. I yield to no one in my appreciation of her *espièglerie*, but I'm one of the rabbits and always have been while she is about as pronounced a dasher as ever dashed. What I like is the quiet life, and Roberta Wickham wouldn't recognize the quiet life if you brought it to her on a plate with watercress round it. She's all for not letting the sun go down without having started something calculated to stagger humanity. In a word, she needs the guiding hand, which is a thing I couldn't supply her with. Whereas from Kipper she will

get it in abundance, he being one of those tough
non-rabbits for whom it is child's play to make the little
woman draw the line somewhere. That is why the union
of these twain has my support and approval and why,
when she told me all that in the pub, I felt like doing a
buck-and-wing dance. Where is Kipper? I should like to
shake him by the hand and pat his back.'

'He went on a picnic with Wilbert and Phyllis.'

The significance of this did not escape me.

'Tailing up stuff, eh? Right on the job, is he?'

'Wilbert is constantly under his eye.'

'And if ever a man needed to be constantly under an
eye, it's the above kleptomaniac.'

'The what?'

'Haven't you been told? Wilbert's a pincher.'

'How do you mean, a pincher?'

'He pinches things. Everything that isn't nailed down
is grist to his mill.'

'Don't be an ass.'

'I'm not being an ass. He's got Uncle Tom's
cow-creamer.'

'I know.'

'You know?'

'Of course I know.'

Her . . . what's the word? . . . phlegm, is it? . . .
something beginning with a p . . . astounded me. I had
expected to freeze her young – or, rather, middle-aged –
blood and have her perm stand on end like quills upon
the fretful porpentine, and she hadn't moved a muscle.

'Beshrew me,' I said, 'you take it pretty calmly.'

'Well, what's there to get excited about? Tom sold
him the thing.'

'What?'

'Wilbert got in touch with him at Harrogate and put
in his bid, and Tom phoned me to give it to him. Just
shows how important that deal must be to Tom. I'd have
thought he would rather have parted with his eyeteeth.'

I drew a deep breath, this time fortunately unmixed with gin and tonic. I was profoundly stirred.

'You mean,' I said, my voice quavering like that of a coloratura soprano, 'that I went through that soul-shattering experience all for nothing?'

'Who's been shattering your soul, if any?'

'Ma Cream. By popping in while I was searching Wilbert's room for the loathsome object. Naturally I thought he'd swiped it and hidden it there.'

'And she caught you?'

'Not once, but twice.'

'What did she say?'

'She recommended me to take treatment from Roddy Glossop, of whose skill in ministering to the mentally afflicted she had heard such good reports. One sees what gave her the idea. I was half-way under the dressing-table at the moment, and no doubt she thought it odd.'

'Bertie! How absolutely priceless!'

The adjective 'priceless' seemed to me an ill-chosen one, and I said so. But my words were lost in the gale of mirth into which she now exploded. I had never heard anyone laugh so heartily, not even Bobbie on the occasion when the rake jumped up and hit me on the tip of the nose.

'I'd have given fifty quid to have been there,' she said, when she was able to get the vocal cords working. 'Half-way under the dressing-table, were you?'

'The second time. When we first forgathered, I was sitting on the floor with a chair round my neck.'

'Like an Elizabethan ruff, as worn by Thomas Botway.'

'Otway,' I said stiffly. As I have mentioned, I like to get things right. And I was about to tell her that what I had hoped for from a blood relation was sympathy and condolence rather than this crackling of thorns under a pot, as it is sometimes called, when the door opened and Bobbie came in.

The moment I cast an eye on her, it seemed to me that there was something strange about her aspect. Normally, this beasel presents to the world the appearance of one who is feeling that if it isn't the best of all possible worlds, it's quite good enough to be going on with till a better one comes along. Verve, I mean, and animation and all that sort of thing. But now there was a listlessness about her, not the listlessness of the cat Augustus but more that of the female in the picture in the Louvre, of whom Jeeves, on the occasion when he lugged me there to take a dekko at her, said that here was the head upon which all the ends of the world are come. He drew my attention, I remember, to the weariness of the eyelids. I got just the same impression of weariness from Bobbie's eyelids.

Unparting her lips which were set in a thin line as if she had just been taking a suck at a lemon, she said:

'I came to get that book of Mrs Cream's that I was reading, Mrs Travers.'

'Help yourself, child,' said the ancestor. 'The more people in this joint reading her stuff, the better. It all goes to help the composition.'

'So you got here all right, Bobbie,' I said. 'Have you seen Kipper?'

I wouldn't say she snorted, but she certainly sniffed.

'Bertie,' she said in a voice straight from the frigidaire, 'will you do me a favour?'

'Of course. What?'

'Don't mention that rat's name in my presence,' she said, and pushed off, the eyelids still weary.

She left me fogged and groping for the inner meaning, and I could see from Aunt Dahlia's goggling eyes that the basic idea hadn't got across with her either.

'Well!' she said. 'What's all this? I thought you told me she loved young Herring with a passion like boiling oil.'

'That was her story.'

'The oil seems to have gone off the boil. Yes, sir, if that was the language of love, I'll eat my hat,' said the blood relation, alluding, I took it, to the beastly straw contraption in which she does her gardening, concerning which I can only say that it is almost as foul as Uncle Tom's Sherlock Holmes deerstalker, which has frightened more crows than any other lid in Worcestershire. 'They must have had a fight.'

'It does look like it,' I agreed, 'and I don't understand how it can have happened considering that she left me with the love light in her eyes and can't have been back here more than about half an hour. What, one asks oneself, in so short a time can have changed a girl full of love and ginger ale into a girl who speaks of the adored object as "that rat" and doesn't want to hear his name mentioned? These are deep waters. Should I send for Jeeves?'

'What on earth can Jeeves do?'

'Well, now you put it that way, I'm bound to admit that I don't know. It's just that one drops into the habit of sending for Jeeves whenever things have gone agley, if that's the word I'm thinking of. Scotch, isn't it? Agley, I mean. It sounds Scotch to me. However, passing lightly over that, the thing to do when you want the low-down is to go to the fountainhead and get it straight from the horse's mouth. Kipper can solve this mystery. I'll pop along and find him.'

I was, however, spared the trouble of popping, for at this moment he entered left centre.

'Oh, there you are, Bertie,' he said. 'I heard you were back. I was looking for you.'

He had spoken in a low, husky sort of way, like a voice from the tomb, and I now saw that he was exhibiting all the earmarks of a man who has recently had a bomb explode in his vicinity. His shoulders sagged and his eyes were glassy. He looked, in short, like the fellow who hadn't started to take Old Doctor Gordon's

Bile Magnesia, and I snapped into it without preamble. This was no time for being tactful and pretending not to notice.

'What's all this strained-relations stuff between you and Bobbie, Kipper?' I said, and when he said, 'Oh, nothing,' rapped the table sharply and told him to cut out the coy stuff and come clean.

'Yes,' said Aunt Dahlia. 'What's happened, young Herring?'

I think for a moment he was about to draw himself up with hauteur and say he would prefer, if we didn't mind, not to discuss his private affairs, but when he was half-way up he caught Aunt Dahlia's eye and returned to position one. Aunt Dahlia's eye, while not in the same class as that of my Aunt Agatha, who is known to devour her young and conduct human sacrifices at the time of the full moon, has lots of authority. He subsided into a chair and sat there looking filleted.

'Well, if you must know,' he said, 'she's broken the engagement.'

This didn't get us any farther. We had assumed as much. You don't go calling people rats if love still lingers.

'But it's only an hour or so,' I said, 'since I left her outside a hostelry called the "Fox and Goose", and she had just been giving you a rave notice. What came unstuck? What did you do to the girl?'

'Oh, nothing.'

'Come, come!'

'Well, it was this way.'

There was a pause here while he said that he would give a hundred quid for a stiff whisky-and-soda, but as this would have involved all the delay of ringing for Pop Glossop and having it fetched from the lowest bin, Aunt Dahlia would have none of it. In lieu of the desired refreshment she offered him a cold crumpet, which he declined, and told him to get on with it.

'Where I went wrong,' he said, still speaking in that low, husky voice as if he had been a ghost suffering from catarrh, 'was in getting engaged to Phyllis Mills.'

'What?' I cried.

'What?' cried Aunt Dahlia.

'Egad!' I said.

'What on earth did you do that for?' said Aunt Dahlia.

He shifted uneasily in his chair, like a man troubled with ants in the pants.

'It seemed a good idea at the time,' he said. 'Bobbie had told me on the telephone that she never wanted to speak to me again in this world or the next, and Phyllis had been telling me that, while she shrank from Wilbert Cream because of his murky past, she found him so magnetic that she knew she wouldn't be able to refuse him if he proposed, and I had been commissioned to stop him proposing, so I thought the simplest thing to do was to get engaged to her myself. So we talked it over, and having reached a thorough understanding that it was simply a ruse and nothing binding on either side, we announced it to Cream.'

'Very shrewd,' said Aunt Dahlia. 'How did he take it?'

'He reeled.'

'Lot of reeling there's been in this business,' I said. 'You reeled, if you recollect, when you remembered you'd written that letter to Bobbie.'

'And I reeled again when she suddenly appeared from nowhere just as I was kissing Phyllis.'

I pursed the lips. Getting a bit French, this sequence, it seemed to me.

'There was no need for you to do that.'

'No need, perhaps, but I wanted to make it look natural to Cream.'

'Oh, I see. Driving it home, as it were?'

'That was the idea. Of course I wouldn't have done it if I'd known that Bobbie had changed her mind and wanted things to be as they were before that telephone conversation. But I didn't know. It's just one of life's little ironies. You get the same sort of thing in Thomas Hardy.'

I knew nothing of this T. Hardy of whom he spoke, but I saw what he meant. It was like what's always happening in the novels of suspense, where the girl goes around saying, 'Had I but known.'

'Didn't you explain?'

He gave me a pitying look.

'Have you ever tried explaining something to a red-haired girl who's madder than a wet hen?'

I took his point.

'What happened then?'

'Oh, she was very lady-like. Talked amiably of this and that till Phyllis had left us. Then she started in. She said she had raced here with a heart overflowing with love, longing to be in my arms, and a jolly surprise it was to find those arms squeezing the stuffing out of another and . . . Oh, well, a lot more along those lines. The trouble is, she's always been a bit squiggle-eyed about Phyllis, because in Switzerland she held the view that we were a shade too matey. Nothing in it, of course.'

'Just good friends?'

'Exactly.'

'Well, if you want to know what I think,' said Aunt Dahlia.

But we never did get around to knowing what she thought, for at this moment Phyllis came in.

13

Giving the wench the once-over as she entered, I found myself well able to understand why Bobbie on observing her entangled with Kipper had exploded with so loud a report. I'm not myself, of course, an idealistic girl in love with a member of the staff of the *Thursday Review* and never have been, but if I were I know I'd get the megrims somewhat severely if I caught him in a clinch with anyone as personable as this stepdaughter of Aubrey Upjohn, for though shaky on the IQ, physically she was a pipterino of the first water. Her eyes were considerably bluer than the skies above, she was wearing a simple summer dress which accentuated rather than hid the graceful outlines of her figure, if you know what I mean, and it was not surprising that Wilbert Cream, seeing her, should have lost no time in reaching for the book of poetry and making a bee line with her to the nearest leafy glade.

'Oh, Mrs Travers,' she said, spotting Aunt Dahlia, 'I've just been talking to Daddy on the telephone.'

This took the old ancestor's mind right off the tangled affairs of the Kipper–Bobbie axis, to which a moment before she had been according her best attention, and I didn't wonder. With the prize-giving at Market Snodsbury Grammar School, a function at which all that was bravest and fairest in the neighbourhood would be present, only two days away, she must have been getting pretty uneasy about the continued absence of the big shot slated to address the young scholars on ideals and life in the world outside. If you are on the board of governors of a school and have contracted to supply an

orator for the great day of the year, you can be forgiven
for feeling a trifle jumpy when you learn that the
silver-tongued one has gadded off to the metropolis,
leaving no word as to when he will be returning, if ever.
For all she knew, Upjohn might have got the holiday
spirit and be planning to remain burning up the
boulevards indefinitely, and of course nothing gives a big
beano a black eye more surely than the failure to show
up of the principal speaker. So now she quite naturally
blossomed like a rose in June and asked if the old son of
a bachelor had mentioned anything about when he was
coming back.

'He's coming back tonight. He says he hopes you
haven't been worrying.'

A snort of about the calibre of an explosion in an
ammunition dump escaped my late father's sister.

'Oh, does he? Well, I've a piece of news for him. I *have*
been worrying. What's kept him in London so long?'

'He's been seeing his lawyer about this libel action
he's bringing against the *Thursday Review*.'

I have often asked myself how many inches it was
that Kipper leaped from his chair at these words.
Sometimes I think it was ten, sometimes only six, but
whichever it was he unquestionably came up from the
padded seat like an athlete competing in the Sitting
High Jump event. Scarface McColl couldn't have risen
more nippily.

'Against the *Thursday Review*?' said Aunt Dahlia.
'That's your rag, isn't it, young Herring? What have they
done to stir him up?'

'It's this book Daddy wrote about preparatory schools.
He wrote a book about preparatory schools. Did you
know he had written a book about preparatory
schools?'

'Hadn't an inkling. Nobody tells me anything.'

'Well, he wrote this book about preparatory schools. It
was about preparatory schools.'

'About preparatory schools, was it?'

'Yes, about preparatory schools.'

'Thank God we've got that straightened out at last. I had a feeling we should get somewhere if we dug long enough. And – ?'

'And the *Thursday Review* said something libellous about it, and Daddy's lawyer says the jury ought to give Daddy at least five thousand pounds. Because they libelled him. So he's been in London all this time seeing his lawyer. But he's coming back tonight. He'll be here for the prize-giving, and I've got his speech all typed out and ready for him. Oh, there's my precious Poppet,' said Phyllis, as a distant barking reached the ears. 'He's asking for his dinner, the sweet little angel. All right, darling, Mother's coming,' she fluted, and buzzed off on the errand of mercy.

A brief silence followed her departure.

'I don't care what you say,' said Aunt Dahlia at length in a defiant sort of way. 'Brains aren't everything. She's a dear, sweet girl. I love her like a daughter, and to hell with anyone who calls her a half-wit. Why, hullo,' she proceeded, seeing that Kipper was slumped back in his chair trying without much success to hitch up a drooping lower jaw. 'What's eating you, young Herring?'

I could see that Kipper was in no shape for conversation, so took it upon myself to explain.

'A certain stickiness has arisen, aged relative. You heard what P. Mills said before going to minister to Poppet. Those words tell the story.'

'What do you mean?'

'The facts are readily stated. Upjohn wrote this slim volume, which, if you recall, was about preparatory schools, and in it, so Kipper tells me, said that the time spent in these establishments was the happiest of our lives. Ye Ed passed it on to Kipper for comment, and he, remembering the dark days at Malvern House, Bramley-on-Sea, when he and I were plucking the

gowans fine there, slated it with no uncertain hand.
Correct, Kipper?'

He found speech, if you could call making a noise like
a buffalo taking its foot out of a swamp finding speech.

'But, dash it,' he said, finding a bit more, 'it was
perfectly legitimate criticism. I didn't mince my words,
of course –'

'It would be interesting to find out what these
unminced words were,' said Aunt Dahlia, 'for among
them there appear to have been one or two which seem
likely to set your proprietor back five thousand of the
best and brightest. Bertie, get your car out and go to
Market Snodsbury station and see if the bookstall has a
copy of this week's . . . No, wait, hold the line. Cancel
that order. I shan't be a minute,' she said, and went out,
leaving me totally fogged as to what she was up to. What
aunts are up to is never an easy thing to divine.

I turned to Kipper.

'Bad show,' I said.

From the way he writhed I gathered that he was
feeling it could scarcely be worse.

'What happens when an editorial assistant on a
weekly paper lets the bosses in for substantial libel
damages?'

He was able to answer that one.

'He gets the push and, what's more, finds it pretty
damned difficult to land another job. He's on the
blacklist.'

I saw what he meant. These birds who run weekly
papers believe in watching the pennies. They like to get
all that's coming to them and when the stuff, instead of
pouring in, starts pouring out as the result of an
injudicious move on the part of a unit of the staff, what
they do to that unit is plenty. I think Kipper's outfit was
financed by some sort of board or syndicate, but boards
and syndicates are just as sensitive about having to
cough up as individual owners. As Kipper had indicated,

they not only give the erring unit the heave-ho but pass
the word round to the other boards and syndicates.

'Herring?' the latter say when Kipper comes seeking
employment. 'Isn't he the bimbo who took the bread out
of the mouths of the *Thursday Review* people? Chuck
the blighter out of the window and we want to see him
bounce.' If this action of Upjohn's went through, his
chances of any sort of salaried post were meagre, if not
slim. It might be years before all was forgiven and
forgotten.

'Selling pencils in the gutter is about the best I'll be
able to look forward to,' said Kipper, and he had just
buried his face in his hands, as fellows are apt to do
when contemplating a future that's a bit on the bleak
side, when the door opened, to reveal not, as I had
expected, Aunt Dahlia, but Bobbie.

'I got the wrong book,' she said. 'The one I wanted
was –'

Then her eye fell on Kipper and she stiffened in every
limb, rather like Lot's wife, who, as you probably know,
did the wrong thing that time there was all that
unpleasantness with the cities of the plain and got
turned into a pillar of salt, though what was the thought
behind this I've never been able to understand. Salt, I
mean. Seems so bizarre somehow and not at all what
you would expect.

'Oh!' she said haughtily, as if offended by this glimpse
into the underworld, and even as she spoke a hollow
groan burst from Kipper's interior and he raised an ashen
face. And at the sight of that ashen f. the haughtiness
went out of Roberta Wickham with a whoosh, to be
replaced by all the old love, sympathy, womanly
tenderness and what not, and she bounded at him like a
leopardess getting together with a lost cub.

'Reggie! Oh, Reggie! Reggie, darling, what is it?' she
cried, her whole demeanour undergoing a marked
change for the better. She was, in short, melted by his

distress, as so often happens with the female sex. Poets have frequently commented on this. You are probably familiar with the one who said 'Oh, woman in our hours of ease tum tumty tiddly something please, when something something something something brow, a something something something thou.'

She turned on me with an animal snarl.

'What have you been doing to the poor lamb?' she demanded, giving me one of the nastiest looks seen that summer in the midland counties, and I had just finished explaining that it was not I but Fate or Destiny that had removed the sunshine from the poor lamb's life, when Aunt Dahlia returned. She had a slip of paper in her hand.

'I was right,' she said. 'I knew Upjohn's first move on getting a book published would be to subscribe to a press-cutting agency. I found this on the hall table. It's your review of his slim volume, young Herring, and having run an eye over it I'm not surprised that he's a little upset. I'll read it to you.'

As might have been expected, this having been foreshadowed a good deal in one way and another, what Kipper had written was on the severe side, and as far as I was concerned it fell into the rare and refreshing fruit class. I enjoyed every minute of it. It concluded as follows:

'Aubrey Upjohn might have taken a different view of preparatory schools if he had done a stretch at the Dotheboys Hall conducted by him at Malvern House, Bramley-on-Sea, as we had the misfortune to do. We have not forgotten the sausages on Sunday, which were made not from contented pigs but from pigs which had expired, regretted by all, of glanders, the botts and tuberculosis.'

Until this passage left the aged relative's lips Kipper had been sitting with the tips of his fingers together, nodding from time to time as much as to say 'Caustic, yes, but perfectly legitimate criticism,' but on hearing this excerpt he did another of his sitting high jumps, lowering all previous records by several inches. It occurred to me as a passing thought that if all other sources of income failed, he had a promising future as an acrobat.

'But I never wrote that,' he gasped.

'Well, it's here in cold print.'

'Why, that's libellous!'

'So Upjohn and his legal eagle seem to feel. And I must say it reads like a pretty good five thousand pounds' worth to me.'

'Let me look at that,' yipped Kipper. 'I don't understand this. No, half a second, darling. Not now. Later. I want to concentrate,' he said, for Bobbie had flung herself on him and was clinging to him like the ivy on the old garden wall.

'Reggie!' she wailed – yes, wail's the word. 'It was me!'

'Eh?'

'That thing Mrs Travers just read. You remember you showed me the proof at lunch that day and told me to drop it off at the office, as you had to rush along to keep a golf date. I read it again after you'd gone, and saw you had left out that bit about the sausages – accidentally, I thought – and it seemed to me so frightfully funny and clever that . . . Well, I put it in at the end. I felt it just rounded the thing off.'

There was silence for some moments, broken only by
the sound of an aunt saying 'Lord love a duck!' Kipper
stood blinking, as I had sometimes seen him do at the
boxing tourneys in which he indulged when in receipt of
a shrewd buffet on some tender spot like the tip of the
nose. Whether or not the idea of taking Bobbie's neck in
both hands and twisting it into a spiral floated through
his mind, I cannot say, but if so it was merely the ideal
dream of a couple of seconds or so, for almost
immediately love prevailed. She had described him as a
lamb, and it was with all the mildness for which lambs
are noted that he now spoke.

'Oh, I see. So that's how it was.'

'I'm so sorry.'

'Don't mention it.'

'Can you ever forgive me?'

'Oh, rather.'

'I meant so well.'

'Of course you did.'

'Will you really get into trouble about this?'

'There may be some slight unpleasantness.'

'Oh, Reggie!'

'Quite all right.'

'I've ruined your life.'

'Nonsense. The *Thursday Review* isn't the only paper
in London. If they fire me, I'll accept employment
elsewhere.'

This scarcely squared with what he had told me about
being blacklisted, but I forbore to mention this, for I saw
that his words had cheered Bobbie up considerably, and I

didn't want to bung a spanner into her mood of *bien être*. Never does to dash the cup of happiness from a girl's lips when after plumbing the depths she has started to take a swig at it.

'Of course!' she said. 'Any paper would be glad to have a valuable man like you.'

'They'll fight like tigers for his services,' I said, helping things along. 'You don't find a chap like Kipper out of circulation for more than a day or so.'

'You're so clever.'

'Oh, thanks.'

'I don't mean you, ass, I mean Reggie.'

'Ah, yes. Kipper has what it takes, all right.'

'All the same,' said Aunt Dahlia, 'I think, when Upjohn arrives, you had better do all you can to ingratiate yourself with him.'

I got her meaning. She was recommending that grappling-to-the-soul-with-hoops-of-steel stuff.

'Yes,' I said. 'Exert the charm, Kipper, and there's a chance he might call the thing off.'

'Bound to,' said Bobbie. 'Nobody can resist you, darling.'

'Do you think so, darling?'

'Of course I do, darling.'

'Well, let's hope you're right, darling. In the meantime,' said Kipper, 'if I don't get that whisky-and-soda soon, I shall disintegrate. Would you mind if I went in search of it, Mrs Travers?'

'It's the very thing I was about to suggest myself. Dash along and drink your fill, my unhappy young stag at eve.'

'I'm feeling rather like a restorative, too,' said Bobbie.

'Me also,' I said, swept along on the tide of the popular movement. 'Though I would advise,' I said, when we were outside, 'making it port. More authority. We'll look in on Swordfish. He will provide.'

We found Pop Glossop in his pantry polishing silver, and put in our order. He seemed a little surprised at the

inrush of such a multitude, but on learning that our
tongues were hanging out obliged with a bottle of the
best, and after we had done a bit of tissue-restoring,
Kipper, who had preserved a brooding silence since
entering, rose and left us, saying that if we didn't mind
he would like to muse apart for a while. I saw Pop
Glossop give him a sharp look as he went out and knew
that Kipper's demeanour had roused his professional
interest, causing him to scent in the young visitor a
potential customer. These brain specialists are always
on the job and never miss a trick. Tactfully waiting till
the door had closed, he said:

'Is Mr Herring an old friend of yours, Mr Wooster?'

'Bertie.'

'I beg your pardon. Bertie. You have known him for
some time?'

'Practically from the egg.'

'And is Miss Wickham a friend of his?'

'Reggie Herring and I are engaged, Sir Roderick,' said
Bobbie. Her words seemed to seal the Glossop lips. He
said 'Oh' and began to talk about the weather and
continued to do so until Bobbie, who since Kipper's
departure had been exhibiting signs of restlessness, said
she thought she would go and see how he was making
out. Finding himself de-Wickham-ed, he unsealed his
lips without delay.

'I did not like to mention it before Miss Wickham, as
she and Mr Herring are engaged, for one is always loath
to occasion anxiety, but that young man has a neurosis.'

'He isn't always as dippy as he looked just now.'

'Nevertheless –'

'And let me tell you something, Roddy. If you were as
up against it as he is, you'd have a neurosis, too.'

And feeling that it would do no harm to get his views
on the Kipper situation, I unfolded the tale.

'So you see the posish,' I concluded. 'The only way he
can avoid the fate that is worse than death – viz. letting

his employers get nicked for a sum beyond the dreams of avarice – is by ingratiating himself with Upjohn, which would seem to any thinking man a shot that's not on the board. I mean, he had four years with him at Malvern House and didn't ingratiate himself once, so it's difficult to see how he's going to start doing it now. It seems to me the thing's an impasse. French expression,' I explained, 'meaning that we're stymied good and proper with no hope of finding a formula.'

To my surprise, instead of clicking the tongue and waggling the head gravely to indicate that he saw the stickiness of the dilemma, he chuckled fatly, as if having spotted an amusing side to the thing which had escaped me. Having done this, he blessed his soul, which was his way of saying 'Gorblimey'.

'It really is quite extraordinary, my dear Bertie,' he said, 'how associating with you restores my youth. Your lightest word seems to bring back old memories. I find myself recollecting episodes in the distant past which I have not thought of for years and years. It is as though you waved a magic wand of some kind. This matter of the problem confronting your friend Mr Herring is a case in point. While you were telling me of his troubles, the mists shredded away, the hands of the clock turned back, and I was once again a young fellow in my early twenties, deeply involved in the strange affair of Bertha Simmons, George Lanchester and Bertha's father, old Mr Simmons, who at that time resided in Putney. He was in the imported lard and butter business.'

'The – what was that strange affair again?'

He repeated the cast of characters, asked me if I would care for another drop of port, a suggestion with which I readily fell in, and proceeded.

'George, a young man of volcanic passions, met Bertha Simmons at a dance at Putney Town Hall in aid of the widows of deceased railway porters and became instantly enamoured. And his love was returned. When he encountered Bertha next day in Putney High Street and, taking her off to a confectioner's for an ice cream, offered her with it his hand and heart, she accepted them enthusiastically. She said that when they were dancing together on the previous night something had seemed to go all over her, and he said he had had exactly the same experience.'

'Twin souls, what?'

'A most accurate description.'

'In fact, so far, so good.'

'Precisely. But there was an obstacle, and a very serious one. George was a swimming instructor at the local baths, and Mr Simmons had higher views for his daughter. He forbade the marriage. I am speaking, of course, of the days when fathers did forbid marriage. It was only when George saved him from drowning that he relented and gave the young couple his consent and blessing.'

'How did that happen?'

'Perfectly simple. I took Mr Simmons for a stroll on the river bank and pushed him in, and George, who was waiting in readiness, dived into the water and pulled him out. Naturally I had to undergo a certain amount of criticism of my clumsiness, and it was many weeks before I received another invitation to Sunday supper at Chatsworth, the Simmons residence, quite a privation in those days when I was a penniless medical student and perpetually hungry, but I was glad to sacrifice myself to help a friend and the results, as far as George was concerned, were of the happiest. And what crossed my mind, as you were telling me of Mr Herring's desire to ingratiate himself with Mr Upjohn, was that a similar – is "set-up" the term you young fellows use? – would answer in his case. All the facilities are here at Brinkley Court. In my rambles about the grounds I have noticed a small but quite adequate lake, and . . . well, there you have it, my dear Bertie. I throw it out, of course, merely as a suggestion.'

His words left me all of a glow. When I thought how I had misjudged him in the days when our relations had been distant, I burned with shame and remorse. It seemed incredible that I could ever have looked on this admirable loony-doctor as the menace in the treatment. What a lesson, I felt, this should teach all of us that a man may have a bald head and bushy eyebrows and still remain at heart a jovial sportsman and one of the boys. There was about an inch of the ruby juice nestling in my glass, and as he finished speaking I raised the beaker in a reverent toast. I told him he had hit the bull's eye and was entitled to a cigar or coconut according to choice.

'I'll go and take the matter up with my principals immediately.'

'Can Mr Herring swim?'

'Like several fishes.'

'Then I see no obstacle in the path.'

We parted with mutual expressions of good will, and it was only after I had emerged into the summer air that I remembered I hadn't told him that Wilbert had purchased, not pinched, the cow-creamer, and for a moment I thought of going back to apprise him. But I thought again, and didn't. First things first, I said to myself, and the item at the top of the agenda paper was the bringing of a new sparkle to Kipper's eyes. Later on, I told myself, would do, and carried on to where he and Bobbie were pacing the lawn with bowed heads. It would not be long, I anticipated, before I would be bringing those heads up with a jerk.

Nor was I in error. Their enthusiasm was unstinted. Both agreed unreservedly that if Upjohn had the merest spark of human feeling in him, which of course had still to be proved, the thing was in the bag.

'But you never thought this up yourself, Bertie,' said

Bobbie, always inclined to underestimate the Wooster shrewdness. 'You've been talking to Jeeves.'

'No, as a matter of fact, it was Swordfish who had the idea.'

Kipper seemed surprised.

'You mean you told him about it?'

'I thought it the strategic move. Four heads are better than three.'

'And he advised shoving Upjohn into the lake?'

'That's right.'

'Rather a peculiar butler.'

I turned this over in my mind.

'Peculiar? Oh, I don't know. Fairly run-of-the-mill I should call him. Yes, more or less the usual type,' I said.

15

With self all eagerness and enthusiasm for the work in
hand, straining at the leash, as you might say, and full of
the will to win, it came as a bit of a damper when I
found on the following afternoon that Jeeves didn't
think highly of Operation Upjohn. I told him about it
just before starting out for the tryst, feeling that it would
be helpful to have his moral support, and was stunned to
see that his manner was austere and even puff-faced. He
was giving me a description at the time of how it felt to
act as judge at a seaside bathing belles contest, and it
was with regret that I was compelled to break into this,
for he had been holding me spellbound.

'I'm sorry, Jeeves,' I said, consulting my watch, 'but I
shall have to be dashing off. Urgent appointment. You
must tell me the rest later.'

'At any time that suits you, sir.'

'Are you doing anything for the next half-hour or so?'

'No, sir.'

'Not planning to curl up in some shady nook with a
cigarette and Spinoza?'

'No, sir.'

'Then I strongly advise you to come down to the lake
and witness a human drama.'

And in a few brief words I outlined the programme
and the events which had led up to it. He listened
attentively and raised his left eyebrow a fraction of an
inch.

'Was this Miss Wickham's idea, sir?'

'No. I agree that it sounds like one of hers, but
actually it was Sir Roderick Glossop who suggested it.

By the way, you were probably surprised to find him buttling here.'

'It did occasion me a momentary astonishment, but Sir Roderick explained the circumstances.'

'Fearing that if he didn't let you in on it, you might unmask him in front of Mrs Cream?'

'No doubt, sir. He would naturally wish to take all precautions. I gathered from his remarks that he has not yet reached a definite conclusion regarding the mental condition of Mr Cream.'

'No, he's still observing. Well, as I say, it was from his fertile bean that the idea sprang. What do you think of it?'

'Ill-advised, sir, in my opinion.'

I was amazed. I could hardly b. my e.

'Ill-advised?'

'Yes, sir.'

'But it worked without a hitch in the case of Bertha Simmons, George Lanchester and old Mr Simmons.'

'Very possibly, sir.'

'Then why this defeatist attitude?'

'It is merely a feeling, sir, due probably to my preference for finesse. I mistrust these elaborate schemes. One cannot depend on them. As the poet Burns says, the best laid plans of mice and men gang aft agley.'

'Scotch, isn't it, that word?'

'Yes, sir.'

'I thought as much. The "gang" told the story. Why do Scotsmen say gang?'

'I have no information, sir. They have not confided in me.'

I was getting a bit peeved by now, not at all liking the sniffiness of his manner. I had expected him to speed me on my way with words of encouragement and uplift, not to go trying to blunt the keen edge of my zest like this. I was rather in the position of a child who runs to his

mother hoping for approval and endorsement of
something he's done, and is awarded instead a brusque
kick in the pants. It was with a good deal of warmth that
I came back at him.

'So you think the poet Burns would look askance at
this enterprise of ours, do you? Well, you can tell him
from me he's an ass. We've thought the thing out to the
last detail. Miss Wickham asks Mr Upjohn to come for a
stroll with her. She leads him to the lake. I am standing
on the brink, ostensibly taking a look at the fishes
playing amongst the reeds. Kipper, ready to the last
button, is behind a neighbouring tree. On the cue "Oh,
look!" from Miss Wickham, accompanied by business of
pointing with girlish excitement at something in the
water, Upjohn bends over to peer. I push, Kipper dives
in, and there we are. Nothing can possibly go wrong.'

'Just as you say, sir. But I still have that feeling.'

The blood of the Woosters is hot, and I was about to
tell him in set terms what I thought of his bally feeling,
when I suddenly spotted what it was that was making
him crab the act. The green-eyed monster had bitten
him. He was miffed because he wasn't the brains behind
this binge, the blue prints for it having been laid down
by a rival. Even great men have their weaknesses. So I
held back the acid crack I might have made, and went
off with a mere 'Oh, yeah?' No sense in twisting the
knife in the wound, I mean.

All the same, I remained a bit hot under the collar,
because when you're all strung up and tense and all that,
the last thing you want is people upsetting you by
bringing in the poet Burns. I hadn't told him, but our
plans had already nearly been wrecked at the outset by
the unfortunate circumstance of Upjohn, while in the
metropolis, having shaved his moustache, this causing
Kipper to come within a toucher of losing his nerve and
calling the whole thing off. The sight of that bare
expanse or steppe of flesh beneath the nose, he said, did

something to him, bringing back the days when he had
so often found his blood turning to ice on beholding it. It
had required quite a series of pep talks to revive his
manly spirits.

However, there was good stuff in the lad, and though
for a while the temperature of his feet had dropped
sharply, threatening to reduce him to the status of a
non-co-operative cat in an adage, at 3.30 Greenwich
Mean Time he was at his post behind the selected tree,
resolved to do his bit. He poked his head round the tree
as I arrived, and when I waved a cheery hand at him,
waved a fairly cheery hand at me. Though I only caught
a glimpse of him, I could see that his upper lip was stiff.

There being no signs as yet of the female star and her
companion, I deduced that I was a bit on the early side. I
lit a cigarette and stood awaiting their entrance, and was
pleased to note that conditions could scarcely have been
better for the coming water fête. Too often on an English
summer day you find the sun going behind the clouds
and a nippy wind springing up from the north-east, but
this afternoon was one of those still, sultry afternoons
when the slightest movement brings the persp. in beads
to the brow, an afternoon, in short, when it would be a
positive pleasure to be shoved into a lake. 'Most
refreshing,' Upjohn would say to himself as the cool
water played about his limbs.

I was standing there running over the stage directions
in my mind to see that I had got them all clear, when I
beheld Wilbert Cream approaching, the dog Poppet
curvetting about his ankles. On seeing me, the hound
rushed forward with uncouth cries as was his wont, but
on heaving alongside and getting a whiff of Wooster
Number Five calmed down, and I was at liberty to
attend to Wilbert, who I could see desired speech with
me.

He was looking, I noticed, fairly green about the gills,
and he conveyed the same suggestion of having just

swallowed a bad oyster which I had observed in Kipper on his arrival at Brinkley. It was plain that the loss of Phyllis Mills, goofy though she unquestionably was, had hit him a shrewd wallop, and I presumed that he was coming to me for sympathy and heart balm, which I would have been only too pleased to dish out. I hoped, of course, that he would make it crisp and remove himself at an early date, for when the moment came for the balloon to go up I didn't want to be hampered by an audience. When you're pushing someone into a lake, nothing embarrasses you more than having the front seats filled up with goggling spectators.

It was not, however, on the subject of Phyllis that he proceeded to touch.

'Oh, Wooster,' he said, 'I was talking to my mother a night or two ago.'

'Oh, yes?' I said, with a slight wave of the hand intended to indicate that if he liked to talk to his mother anywhere, all over the house, he had my approval.

'She tells me you are interested in mice.'

I didn't like the trend the conversation was taking, but I preserved my aplomb.

'Why, yes, fairly interested.'

'She says she found you trying to catch one in my bedroom!'

'Yes, that's right.'

'Good of you to bother.'

'Not at all. Always a pleasure.'

'She says you seemed to be making a very thorough search of my room.'

'Oh, well, you know, when one sets one's hand to the plough.'

'You didn't find a mouse?'

'No, no mouse. Sorry.'

'I wonder if by any chance you happened to find an eighteenth-century cow-creamer?'

'Eh?'

'A silver jug shaped like a cow.'

'No. Why, was it on the floor somewhere?'

'It was in a drawer of the bureau.'

'Ah, then I would have missed it.'

'You'd certainly miss it now. It's gone.'

'Gone?'

'Gone.'

'You mean disappeared, as it were?'

'I do.'

'Strange.'

'Very strange.'

'Yes, does seem extremely strange, doesn't it?'

I had spoken with all the old Wooster coolness, and I doubt if a casual observer would have detected that Bertram was not at his ease, but I can assure my public that he wasn't by a wide margin. My heart had leaped in the manner popularized by Kipper Herring and Scarface McColl, crashing against my front teeth with a thud which must have been audible in Market Snodsbury. A far less astute man would have been able to divine what had happened. Not knowing the score owing to having missed the latest stop-press news and looking on the cow-creamer purely in the light of a bit of the swag collected by Wilbert in the course of his larcenous career, Pop Glossop, all zeal, had embarked on the search he had planned to make, and intuition, developed by years of hunt-the-slipper, had led him to the right spot. Too late I regretted sorely that, concentrating so tensely on Operation Upjohn, I had failed to place the facts before him. Had he but known, about summed it up.

'I was going to ask you,' said Wilbert, 'if you think I should inform Mrs Travers.'

The cigarette I was smoking was fortunately one of the kind that make you nonchalant, so it was nonchalantly – or fairly nonchalantly – that I was able to reply.

'Oh, I wouldn't do that.'

'Why not?'

'Might upset her.'

'You consider her a sensitive plant?'

'Oh, very. Rugged exterior, of course, but you can't go by that. No, I'd just wait a while, if I were you. I expect it'll turn out that the thing's somewhere you put it but didn't think you'd put it. I mean, you often put a thing somewhere and think you've put it somewhere else and then find you didn't put it somewhere else but somewhere. I don't know if you follow me?'

'I don't.'

'What I mean is, just stick around and you'll probably find the thing.'

'You think it will return?'

'I do.'

'Like a homing pigeon?'

'That's the idea.'

'Oh?' said Wilbert, and turned away to greet Bobbie and Upjohn, who had just arrived on the boat-house landing stage. I had found his manner a little peculiar, particularly that last 'Oh?' but I was glad that there was no lurking suspicion in his mind that I had taken the bally thing. He might so easily have got the idea that Uncle Tom, regretting having parted with his ewe lamb, had employed me to recover it privily, this being the sort of thing, I believe, that collectors frequently do. Nevertheless, I was still much shaken, and I made a mental note to tell Roddy Glossop to slip it back among his effects at the earliest possible moment.

I shifted over to where Bobbie and Upjohn were standing, and though up and doing with a heart for any fate couldn't help getting that feeling you get at times like this of having swallowed a double portion of butterflies. My emotions were somewhat similar to those I had experienced when I first sang the Yeoman's Wedding Song. In public, I mean, for of course I had long been singing it in my bath.

'Hullo, Bobbie,' I said.

'Hullo, Bertie,' she said.

'Hullo, Upjohn,' I said.

The correct response to this would have been 'Hullo, Wooster', but he blew up in his lines and merely made a noise like a wolf with its big toe caught in a trap. Seemed a bit restive, I thought, as if wishing he were elsewhere.

Bobbie was all girlish animation.

'I've been telling Mr Upjohn about that big fish we saw in the lake yesterday, Bertie.'

'Ah yes, the big fish.'

'It was a whopper, wasn't it?'

'Very well-developed.'

'I brought him down here to show it to him.'

'Quite right. You'll enjoy the big fish, Upjohn.'

I had been perfectly correct in supposing him to be restive. He did his wolf impersonation once more.

'I shall do nothing of the sort,' he said, and you couldn't find a better word than 'testily' to describe the way he spoke. 'It is most inconvenient for me to be away from the house at this time. I am expecting a telephone call from my lawyer.'

'Oh, I wouldn't bother about telephone calls from lawyers,' I said heartily. 'These legal birds never say anything worth listening to. Just gab gab gab. You'll never forgive yourself if you miss the big fish. You were saying, Upjohn?' I broke off courteously, for he had spoken.

'I am saying, Mr Wooster, that both you and Miss Wickham are labouring under a singular delusion in supposing that I am interested in fish, whether large or small. I ought never to have left the house. I shall return there at once.'

'Oh, don't go yet,' I said.

'Wait for the big fish,' said Bobbie.

'Bound to be along shortly,' I said.

'At any moment now,' said Bobbie.

Her eyes met mine, and I read in them the message she was trying to convey – viz. that the time had come to act. There is a tide in the affairs of men which taken at the flood leads on to fortune. Not my own. Jeeves's. She bent over and pointed with an eager finger.

'Oh, look!' she cried.

This, as I had explained to Jeeves, should have been the cue for Upjohn to bend over, too, thus making it a simple task for me to do my stuff, but he didn't bend over an inch. And why? Because at this moment the goof Phyllis, suddenly appearing in our midst, said:

'Daddy, dear, you're wanted on the telephone.'

Upon which, standing not on the order of his going, Upjohn was off as if propelled from a gun. He couldn't have moved quicker if he had been the dachshund Poppet, who at this juncture was running round in circles, trying, if I read his thoughts aright, to work off the rather heavy lunch he had had earlier in the afternoon.

One began to see what the poet Burns had meant. I don't know anything that more promptly gums up a dramatic sequence than the sudden and unexpected exit of an important member of the cast at a critical point in the proceedings. I was reminded of the time when we did *Charley's Aunt* at the Market Snodsbury Town Hall in aid of the local church organ fund and half-way through the second act, just when we were all giving of our best, Catsmeat Potter-Pirbright, who was playing Lord Fancourt Babberley, left the stage abruptly to attend to an unforeseen nose bleed.

As far as Bobbie and I were concerned, silence reigned, this novel twist in the scenario having wiped speech from our lips, as the expression is, but Phyllis continued vocal.

'I found this darling pussycat in the garden,' she said, and for the first time I observed that she was bearing

Augustus in her arms. He was looking a bit disgruntled, and one could readily see why. He wanted to catch up with his sleep and was being kept awake by the endearments she was murmuring in his ear.

She lowered him to the ground.

'I brought him here to talk to Poppet. Poppet loves cats, don't you angel? Come and say how-d'you-do to the sweet pussykins, darling.'

I shot a quick look at Wilbert Cream, to see how he was reacting to this. It was the sort of observation which might well have quenched the spark of love in his bosom, for nothing tends to cool the human heart more swiftly than babytalk. But so far from being revolted he was gazing yearningly at her as if her words were music to his ears. Very odd, I felt, and I was just saying to myself that you never could tell, when I became aware of a certain liveliness in my immediate vicinity.

At the moment when Augustus touched ground and curling himself into a ball fell into a light doze, Poppet had completed his tenth lap and was preparing to start on his eleventh. Seeing Augustus, he halted in mid-stride, smiled broadly, turned his ears inside out, stuck his tail straight up at right angles to the parent body and bounded forward, barking merrily.

I could have told the silly ass his attitude was all wrong. Roused abruptly from slumber, the most easy-going cat is apt to wake up cross. Already Augustus had had much to endure from Phyllis, who had doubtless jerked him out of dreamland when scooping him up in the garden, and all this noise and heartiness breaking out just as he dropped off again put the lid on his sullen mood. He spat peevishly, there was a sharp yelp, and something long and brown came shooting between my legs, precipitating itself and me into the depths. The waters closed about me, and for an instant I knew no more.

When I rose to the surface, I found that Poppet and I

were not the only bathers. We had been joined by
Wilbert Cream, who had dived in, seized the hound by
the scruff of the neck, and was towing him at a brisk
pace to the shore. And by one of those odd coincidences
I was at this moment seized by the scruff of the neck
myself.

'It's all right, Mr Upjohn, keep quite cool, keep quite
. . . What the hell are you doing here, Bertie?' said
Kipper, for it was he. I may have been wrong, but it
seemed to me that he spoke petulantly.

I expelled a pint or so of H_2O.

'You may well ask,' I said, moodily detaching a water
beetle from my hair. 'I don't know if you know the
meaning of the word "agley", Kipper, but that, to put it
in a nutshell, is the way things have ganged.'

16

Reaching the mainland some moments later and squelching back to the house, accompanied by Bobbie, like a couple of Napoleons squelching back from Moscow, we encountered Aunt Dahlia, who, wearing that hat of hers that looks like one of those baskets you carry fish in, was messing about in the herbaceous border by the tennis lawn. She gaped at us dumbly for perhaps five seconds, then uttered an ejaculation, far from suitable to mixed company, which she had no doubt picked up from fellow-Nimrods in her hunting days. Having got this off the chest, she said:

'What's been going on in this joint? Wilbert Cream came by here just now, soaked to the eyebrows, and now you two appear, leaking at every seam. Have you all been playing water polo with your clothes on?'

'Not so much water polo, more that seaside bathing belles stuff,' I said. 'But it's a long story, and one feels that the cagey thing for Kipper and me to do now is to nip along and get into some dry things, not to linger conferring with you, much,' I added courteously, 'as we always enjoy your conversation.'

'The extraordinary thing is that I saw Upjohn not long ago, and he was as dry as a bone. How was that? Couldn't you get him to play with you?'

'He had to go and talk to his lawyer on the phone,' I said, and leaving Bobbie to place the facts before her, we resumed our squelching. And I was in my room, having shed the moistened outer crust and substituted something a bit more *sec* in pale flannel, when there was a knock on the door. I flung wide the gates and found Bobbie and Kipper on the threshold.

The first thing I noticed about their demeanour was the strange absence of gloom, despondency and what not. I mean, considering that it was little more than a quarter of an hour since all our hopes and dreams had taken the knock, one would have expected their hearts to be bowed down with weight of woe, but their whole aspect was one of buck and optimism. It occurred to me as a possible solution that with that bulldog spirit of never admitting defeat which has made Englishmen – and, of course, Englishwomen – what they are they had decided to have another go along the same lines at some future date, and I asked if this was the case.

The answer was in the negative. Kipper said No, there was no likelihood of getting Upjohn down to the lake again, and Bobbie said that even if they did, it wouldn't be any good, because I would be sure to mess things up once more.

This stung me, I confess.

'How do you mean, mess things up?'

'You'd be bound to trip over your flat feet and fall in, as you did today.'

'Pardon me,' I said, preserving with an effort the polished suavity demanded from an English gentleman when chewing the rag with one of the other sex, 'you're talking through the back of your fatheaded little neck. I did not trip over my flat feet. I was hurled into the depths by an Act of God, to wit, a totally unexpected dachshund getting between my legs. If you're going to blame anyone blame the goof Phyllis for bringing Augustus there and calling him in his hearing a sweet pussykins. Naturally it made him sore and disinclined to stand any lip from barking dogs.'

'Yes,' said Kipper, always the staunch pal. 'It wasn't Bertie's fault, angel. Say what you will of dachshunds, their peculiar shape makes them the easiest breed of dog to trip over in existence. I feel that Bertie emerges without a stain on his character.'

'I don't,' said Bobbie. 'Still, it doesn't matter.'

'No, it doesn't really matter,' said Kipper, 'because your aunt has suggested a scheme that's just as good as the Lanchester–Simmons thing, if not better. She was telling Bobbie about the time when Boko Fittleworth was trying to ingratiate himself with your Uncle Percy, and you very sportingly offered to go and call your Uncle Percy a lot of offensive names, so that Boko, hovering outside the door, could come in and stick up for him, thus putting himself in solid with him. You probably remember the incident?'

I quivered. I remembered the incident all right.

'She thinks the same treatment would work with Upjohn, and I'm sure she's right. You know how you feel when you suddenly discover you've a real friend, a fellow who thinks you're terrific and won't hear a word said against you. It touches you. If you had anything in the nature of a prejudice against the chap, you change your opinion of him. You feel you can't do anything to injure such a sterling bloke. And that's how Upjohn is going to feel about me, Bertie, when I come in and lend him my sympathy and support as you stand there calling him all the names you can think of. You must have picked up dozens from your aunt. She used to hunt, and if you hunt, you have to know all the names there are because people are always riding over hounds and all that. Ask her to jot down a few of the best on a half-sheet of notepaper.'

'He won't need that,' said Bobbie. 'He's probably got them all tucked away in his mind.'

'Of course. Learned them at her knee as a child. Well, that's the set-up, Bertie. You wait your opportunity and corner Upjohn somewhere and tower over him –'

'As he crouches in his chair.'

'– and shake your finger in his face and abuse him roundly. And when he's quailing beneath your scorn and wishing some friend in need would intervene and save him from this terrible ordeal, I come in, having heard all. Bobbie suggests that I knock you down, but I don't think I could do that. The recollection of our ancient friendship would make me pull my punch. I shall simply rebuke you. "Wooster," I shall say, "I am shocked. Shocked and astounded. I cannot understand how you can talk like that to a man I have always respected and looked up to, a man in whose preparatory school I spent the happiest years of my life. You strangely forget yourself, Wooster." Upon which, you slink out, bathed in shame and confusion, and Upjohn thanks me brokenly and says if there is anything he can do for me, I have only to name it.'

'I still think you ought to knock him down.'

'Having endeared myself to him thus –'

'Much more box-office.'

'Having endeared myself to him thus, I lead the conversation round to the libel suit.'

'One good punch in the eye would do it.'

'I say that I have seen the current issue of the *Thursday Review*, and I can quite understand him wanting to mulct the journal in substantial damages, but "Don't forget, Mr Upjohn," I say, "that when a weekly paper loses a chunk of money, it has to retrench, and the way it retrenches is by getting rid of the more junior members of its staff. You wouldn't want me to lose my job, would you, Mr Upjohn?" He starts. "Are you on the staff of the *Thursday Review*?" he says. "For the time being, yes," I say. "But if you bring that suit, I shall be selling pencils in the street." This is the crucial moment. Looking into his eyes, I can see that he is thinking of that five thousand quid, and for an instant quite naturally he hesitates. Then his better self prevails. His eyes soften. They fill with tears. He clasps my hand. He tells me he could use five thousand quid as well as the next man, but no money in the world would make him dream of doing an injury to the fellow who championed him so stoutly against the louse Wooster, and the scene ends with our going off together to Swordfish's pantry for a drop of port, probably with our arms round each other's waists, and that night he writes a letter to his lawyer telling him to call the suit off. Any questions?'

'Not from me. It isn't as if he could find out that it was you who wrote that review. It wasn't signed.'

'No, thank heaven for the editorial austerity that prevented that.'

'I can't see a flaw in the scenario. He'll have to withdraw the suit.'

'In common decency, one would think. The only thing that remains is to choose a time and place for Bertie to operate.'

'No time like the present.'

'But how do we locate Upjohn?'

'He's in Mr Travers's study. I saw him through the french window.'

'Excellent. Then, Bertie, if you're ready . . .'

It will probably have been noticed that during these exchanges I had taken no part in the conversation. This was because I was fully occupied with envisaging the horror that lay before me. I knew that it did lie before me, of course, for where the ordinary man would have met the suggestion they had made with a firm *nolle prosequi*, I was barred from doing this by the code of the Woosters, which, as is pretty generally known, renders it impossible for me to let a pal down. If the only way of saving a boyhood friend from having to sell pencils in the street – though I should have thought that blood oranges would have been a far more lucrative line – was by wagging my finger in the face of Aubrey Upjohn and calling him names, that finger would have to be wagged and those names called. The ordeal would whiten my hair from the roots up and leave me a mere shell of my former self, but it was one that I must go through. Mine not to reason why, as the fellow said.

So I uttered a rather husky 'Right-ho' and tried not to think of how the Upjohn face looked without its moustache. For what chilled the feet most was the mental picture of that bare upper lip which he had so often twitched at me in what are called days of yore. Dimly, as we started off for the arena, I could hear Bobbie saying 'My hero!' and Kipper asking anxiously if I was in good voice, but it would have taken a fat lot more than my-hero-ing and solicitude about my vocal cords to restore tone to Bertram's nervous system. I was, in short, feeling like an inexperienced novice going up against the heavyweight champion when in due course I drew up at the study door, opened it and tottered in. I could not forget that an Aubrey Upjohn who for years had been looking strong parents in the eye and making them wilt, and whose toughness was a byword in Bramley-on-Sea, was not a man lightly to wag a finger in the face of.

Uncle Tom's study was a place I seldom entered during my visits to Brinkley Court, because when I did go there he always grabbed me and started to talk about old silver, whereas if he caught me in the open he often touched on other topics, and the way I looked at it was that there was no sense in sticking one's neck out. It was more than a year since I had been inside this sanctum, and I had forgotten how extraordinarily like its interior was to that of Aubrey Upjohn's lair at Malvern House. Discovering this now and seeing Aubrey Upjohn seated at the desk as I had so often seen him sit on the occasions when he had sent for me to discuss some recent departure of mine from the straight and narrow path, I found what little was left of my sang froid expiring with a pop. And at the same time I spotted the flaw in this scheme I had undertaken to sit in on – viz.

that you can't just charge into a room and start calling someone names – out of a blue sky, as it were – you have to lead up to the thing. Pourparlers, in short, are of the essence.

So I said 'Oh, hullo,' which seemed to me about as good a pourparler as you could have by way of an opener. I should imagine that those statesmen of whom I was speaking always edge into their conferences conducted in an atmosphere of the utmost cordiality in some such manner.

'Reading?' I said.

He lowered his book – one of Ma Cream's, I noticed – and flashed an upper lip at me.

'Your powers of observation have not led you astray, Wooster. I *am* reading.'

'Interesting book?'

'Very. I am counting the minutes until I can resume its perusal undisturbed.'

I'm pretty quick, and I at once spotted that the atmosphere was not of the utmost cordiality. He hadn't spoken matily, and he wasn't eyeing me matily. His whole manner seemed to suggest that he felt that I was taking up space in the room which could have been better employed for other purposes.

However, I persevered.

'I see you've shaved off your moustache.'

'I have. You do not feel, I hope, that I pursued a mistaken course?'

'Oh no, rather not. I grew a moustache myself last year, but had to get rid of it.'

'Indeed?'

'Public sentiment was against it.'

'I see. Well, I should be delighted to hear more of your reminiscences, Wooster, but at the moment I am expecting a telephone call from my lawyer.'

'I thought you'd had one.'

'I beg your pardon?'

'When you were down by the lake, didn't you go off to talk to him?'

'I did. But when I reached the telephone, he had grown tired of waiting and had rung off. I should never have allowed Miss Wickham to take me away from the house.'

'She wanted you to see the big fish.'

'So I understood her to say.'

'Talking of fish, you must have been surprised to find Kipper here.'

'Kipper?'

'Herring.'

'Oh, Herring,' he said, and one spotted the almost total lack of animation in his voice. And conversation had started to flag, when the door flew open and the goof Phyllis bounded in, full of girlish excitement.

'Oh, Daddy,' she burbled, 'are you busy?'

'No, my dear.'

'Can I speak to you about something?'

'Certainly. Goodbye, Wooster.'

I saw what this meant. He didn't want me around. There was nothing for it but to ooze out through the french window, so I oozed, and had hardly got outside when Bobbie sprang at me like a leopardess.

'What on earth are you fooling about for like this, Bertie?' she stage-whispered. 'All that rot about moustaches. I thought you'd be well into it by this time.'

I pointed out that as yet Aubrey Upjohn had not given me a cue.

'You and your cues!'

'All right, me and my cues. But I've got to sort of lead the conversation in the right direction, haven't I?'

'I see what Bertie means, darling,' said Kipper. 'He wants –'

'A *point d'appui*.'

'A what?' said Bobbie.

'Sort of jumping-off place.'

The beasel snorted.

'If you ask me, he's lost his nerve. I knew this would happen. The worm has got cold feet.'

I could have crushed her by drawing her attention to the fact that worms don't have feet, cold or piping hot, but I had no wish to bandy words.

'I must ask you, Kipper,' I said with frigid dignity, 'to request your girl friend to preserve the decencies of debate. My feet are not cold. I am as intrepid as a lion and only too anxious to get down to brass tacks, but just as I was working round to the *res*, Phyllis came in. She said she had something she wanted to speak to him about.'

Bobbie snorted again, this time in a despairing sort of way.

'She'll be there for hours. It's no good waiting.'

'No,' said Kipper. 'May as well call it off for the moment. We'll let you know time and place of next fixture, Bertie.'

'Oh, thanks,' I said, and they drifted away.

And about a couple of minutes later, as I stood there brooding on Kipper's sad case, Aunt Dahlia came along. I was glad to see her. I thought she might possibly come across with aid and comfort, for though, like the female in the poem I was mentioning, she sometimes inclined to be a toughish egg in hours of ease, she could generally be relied on to be there with the soothing solace when one had anything wrong with one's brow.

As she approached, I got the impression that her own brow had for some reason taken it on the chin. Quite a good deal of that upon-which-all-the-ends-of-the-earth-are-come stuff, it seemed to me.

Nor was I mistaken.

'Bertie,' she said, heaving to beside me and waving a trowel in an overwrought manner, 'do you know what?'

'No, what?'

'I'll tell you what,' said the aged relative, rapping out a sharp monosyllable such as she might have uttered in her Quorn and Pytchley days on observing a unit of the pack of hounds chasing a rabbit. 'That ass Phyllis has gone and got engaged to Wilbert Cream!'

17

Her words gave me quite a wallop. I don't say I reeled, and everything didn't actually go black, but I was shaken, as what nephew would not have been. When a loved aunt has sweated herself to the bone trying to save her god-child from the clutches of a New York playboy and learns that all her well-meant efforts have gone blue on her, it's only natural for her late brother's son to shudder in sympathy.

'You don't mean that?' I said. 'Who told you?'

'She did.'

'In person?'

'In the flesh. She came skipping to me just now, clapping her little hands and bleating about how very, very happy she was, dear Mrs Travers. The silly young geezer. I nearly conked her one with my trowel. I'd always thought her half-baked, but now I think they didn't even put her in the oven.'

'But how did it happen?'

'Apparently that dog of hers joined you in the water.'

'Yes, that's right, he took his dip with the rest of us. But what's that got to do with it?'

'Wilbert Cream dived in and saved him.'

'He could have got ashore perfectly well under his own steam. In fact, he was already on his way, doing what looked like an Australian crawl.'

'That wouldn't occur to a pinhead like Phyllis. To her Wilbert Cream is the man who rescued her dachshund from a watery grave. So she's going to marry him.'

'But you don't marry fellows because they rescue dachshunds.'

'You do, if you've a mentality like hers.'

'Seems odd.'

'And is. But that's how it goes. Girls like Phyllis Mills are an open book to me. For four years I was, if you remember, the proprietor and editress of a weekly paper for women.' She was alluding to the periodical entitled *Milady's Boudoir*, to the Husbands and Brothers page of which I once contributed an article or 'piece' on What The Well-Dressed Man Is Wearing. It had recently been sold to a mug up Liverpool way, and I have never seen Uncle Tom look chirpier than when the deal went through, he for those four years having had to foot the bills.

'I don't suppose,' she continued, 'that you were a regular reader, so for your information there appeared in each issue a short story, and in seventy per cent of those short stories the hero won the heroine's heart by saving her dog or her cat or her canary or whatever foul animal she happened to possess. Well, Phyllis didn't write all those stories, but she easily might have done, for that's the way her mind works. When I say mind,' said the blood relation, 'I refer to the quarter-teaspoonful of brain which you might possibly find in her head if you sank an artesian well. Poor Jane!'

'Poor who?'

'Her mother. Jane Mills.'

'Oh, ah, yes. She was a pal of yours, you told me.'

'The best I ever had, and she was always saying to me "Dahlia, old girl, if I pop off before you, for heaven's sake look after Phyllis and see that she doesn't marry some ghastly outsider. She's sure to want to. Girls always do, goodness knows why," she said, and I knew she was thinking of her first husband, who was a heel to end all heels and a constant pain in the neck to her till one night he most fortunately walked into the River Thames while under the influence of the sauce and didn't come up for days. "Do stop her," she said, and I said "Jane, you can rely on me." And now this happens.'

I endeavoured to soothe.

'You can't blame yourself.'

'Yes, I can.'

'It isn't your fault.'

'I invited Wilbert Cream here.'

'Merely from a wifely desire to do Uncle Tom a bit of good.'

'And I let Upjohn stick around, always at her elbow egging her on.'

'Yes, Upjohn's the bird I blame.'

'Me, too.'

'But for his – undue influence, do they call it? – Phyllis would have remained a bachelor or spinster or whatever it is. "Thou art the man, Upjohn!" seems to me the way to sum it up. He ought to be ashamed of himself.'

'And am I going to tell him so! I'd give a tenner to have Aubrey Upjohn here at this moment.'

'You can get him for nothing. He's in Uncle Tom's study.'

Her face lit up.

'He is?' She threw her head back and inflated the lungs. 'UPJOHN!' she boomed, rather like someone calling the cattle home across the sands of Dee, and I issued a kindly word of warning.

'Watch that blood pressure, old ancestor.'

'Never you mind my blood pressure. You let it alone, and it'll leave you alone. UPJOHN!'

He appeared in the french window, looking cold and severe, as I had so often seen him look when hobnobbing with him in his study at Malvern House, self not there as a willing guest but because I'd been sent for. ('I should like to see Wooster in my study immediately after morning prayers' was the formula.)

'Who is making that abominable noise? Oh, it's you, Dahlia.'

'Yes, it's me.'

'You wished to see me?'

'Yes, but not the way you're looking now. I'd have preferred you to have fractured your spine or at least to have broken a couple of ankles and got a touch of leprosy.'

'My dear Dahlia!'

'I'm not your dear Dahlia. I'm a seething volcano. Have you seen Phyllis?'

'She has just left me.'

'Did she tell you?'

'That she was engaged to Wilbert Cream? Certainly.'

'And I suppose you're delighted?'

'Of course I am.'

'Yes, of course you are! I can well imagine that it's your dearest wish to see that unfortunate muttonheaded girl become the wife of a man who lets off stink bombs in night clubs and pinches the spoons and has had three divorces already and who, if the authorities play their cards right, will end up cracking rocks in Sing-Sing. That is unless the loony-bin gets its bid in first. Just a Prince Charming, you might say.'

'I don't understand you.'

'Then you're an ass.'

'Well, really!' said Aubrey Upjohn, and there was a dangerous note in his voice. I could see that the relative's manner, which was not affectionate, and her words, which lacked cordiality, were peeving him. It looked like an odds-on shot that in about another two ticks he would be giving her the Collect for the Day to write out ten times or even instructing her to bend over while he fetched his whangee. You can push these preparatory schoolmasters just so far.

'A fine way for Jane's daughter to end up. Mrs Broadway Willie!'

'Broadway Willie?'

'That's what he's called in the circles in which he moves, into which he will now introduce Phyllis. "Meet the moll," he'll say, and then he'll teach her in twelve easy lessons how to make stink bombs, and the children, if and when, will be trained to pick people's pockets as they dandle them on their knee. And you'll be responsible, Aubrey Upjohn!'

I didn't like the way things were trending. Admittedly the aged relative was putting up a great show and it was a pleasure to listen to her, but I had seen Upjohn's lip twitch and that look of smug satisfaction come into his face which I had so often seen when he had been counsel for the prosecution in some case in which I was involved and had spotted a damaging flaw in my testimony. The occasion when I was on trial for having broken the drawing-room window with a cricket ball springs to the mind. It was plain to an eye as discerning as mine that he was about to put it across the old flesh-and-blood properly, making her wish she hadn't spoken. I couldn't see how, but the symptoms were all there.

I was right. That twitching lip had not misled me.

'If I might be allowed to make a remark, my dear Dahlia,' he said, 'I think we are talking at cross purposes. You appear to be under the impression that Phyllis is marrying Wilbert's younger brother Wilfred, the notorious playboy whose escapades have caused the family so much distress and who, as you are correct in saying, is known to his disreputable friends as Broadway Willie. Wilfred, I agree, would make – and on three successive occasions has made – a most undesirable husband, but no one to my knowledge has ever spoken a derogatory word of Wilbert. I know few young men who are more generally respected. He is a member of the faculty of one of the greatest American universities, over in this country on his sabbatical. He teaches romance languages.'

Stop me if I've told you this before, I rather fancy I have, but once when I was up at Oxford and chatting on the river bank with a girl called something that's slipped my mind there was a sound of barking and a great hefty dog of the Hound of the Baskervilles type came galloping at me, obviously intent on mayhem, its whole aspect that of a dog that has no use for Woosters. And I was just commending my soul to God and thinking that this was where my new flannel trousers got about thirty bobs' worth of value bitten out of them, when the girl, waiting till she saw the whites of its eyes, with extraordinary presence of mind opened a coloured Japanese umbrella in the animal's face. Upon which, with a startled exclamation it did three back somersaults and retired into private life.

And the reason I bring this up now is that, barring the somersaults, Aunt Dahlia's reaction to this communiqué was precisely that of the above hound to the Japanese umbrella. The same visible taken-abackness. She has since told me that her emotions were identical with those she had experienced when she was out with the Pytchley and riding over a ploughed field in rainy weather, and the horse of a sports-lover in front of her suddenly kicked three pounds of wet mud into her face.

She gulped like a bulldog trying to swallow a sirloin steak many sizes too large for its thoracic cavity.

'You mean there are two of them?'

'Exactly.'

'And Wilbert isn't the one I thought he was?'

'You have grasped the position of affairs to a nicety. You will appreciate now, my dear Dahlia,' said Upjohn, speaking with the same unction, if that's the word, with which he had spoken when unmasking his batteries and presenting unshakable proof that yours was the hand, Wooster, which propelled this cricket ball, 'that your concern, though doing you the greatest credit, has been needless. I could wish Phyllis no better husband. Wilbert has looks, brains, character . . . and excellent prospects,' he added, rolling the words round his tongue like vintage port. 'His father, I should imagine, would be worth at least twenty million dollars, and Wilbert is the elder son. Yes, most satisfactory, most . . .'

As he spoke, the telephone rang, and with a quick 'Ha!' he shot back into the study like a homing rabbit.

18

For perhaps a quarter of a minute after he had passed from the scene the aged relative stood struggling for utterance. At the end of this period she found speech.

'Of all the damn silly fatheaded things!' she vociferated, if that's the word. 'With a million ruddy names to choose from, these ruddy Creams call one ruddy son Wilbert and the other ruddy son Wilfred, and both these ruddy sons are known as Willie. Just going out of their way to mislead the innocent bystander. You'd think people would have more consideration.'

Again I begged her to keep an eye on her blood pressure and not get so worked up, and once more she brushed me off, this time with a curt request that I would go and boil my head.

'You'd be worked up if you had just been scored off by Aubrey Upjohn, with that loathsome self-satisfied look on his face as if he'd been rebuking a pimply pupil at his beastly school for shuffling his feet in church.'

'Odd, that,' I said, struck by the coincidence. 'He once rebuked me for that very reason. And I had pimples.'

'Pompous ass!'

'Shows what a small world it is.'

'What's he doing here anyway? I didn't invite him.'

'Bung him out. I took this point up with you before, if you remember. Cast him into the outer darkness, where there is wailing and gnashing of teeth.'

'I will, if he gives me any more of his lip.'

'I can see you're in a dangerous mood.'

'You bet I'm in a dangerous . . . My God! He's with us again!'

And A. Upjohn was indeed filtering through the french window. But he had lost the look of which the ancestor had complained, the one he was wearing now seeming to suggest that since last heard from something had occurred to wake the fiend that slept in him.

'Dahlia!' he . . . yes better make it vociferated once more, I'm pretty sure it's the word I want.

The fiend that slept in Aunt Dahlia was also up on its toes. She gave him a look which, if directed at an erring member of the personnel of the Quorn or Pytchley hound ensemble, would have had that member sticking his tail between his legs and resolving for the future to lead a better life.

'Now what?'

Just as Aunt Dahlia had done, Aubrey Upjohn struggled for utterance. Quite a bit of utterance-struggling there had been around these parts this summer afternoon.

'I have just been speaking to my lawyer on the telephone,' he said, getting going after a short stage wait. 'I had asked him to make inquiries and ascertain the name of the author of that libellous attack on me in the columns of the *Thursday Review*. He did so, and has now informed me that it was the work of my former pupil, Reginald Herring.'

He paused at this point, to let us chew it over, and the heart sank. Mine, I mean. Aunt Dahlia's seemed to be carrying on much as usual. She scratched her chin with her trowel, and said:

'Oh, yes?'

Upjohn blinked, as if he had been expecting something better than this in the way of sympathy and concern.

'Is that all you can say?'

'That's the lot.'

'Oh? Well, I am suing the paper for heavy damages, and furthermore, I refuse to remain in the same house with Reginald Herring. Either he goes, or I go.'

There was the sort of silence which I believe cyclones drop into for a second or two before getting down to it and starting to give the populace the works. Throbbing? Yes, throbbing wouldn't be a bad word to describe it. Nor would electric, for the matter of that, and if you care to call it ominous, it will be all right with me. It was a silence of the type that makes the toes curl and sends a shiver down the spinal cord as you stand waiting for the bang. I could see Aunt Dahlia swelling slowly like a chunk of bubble gum, and a less prudent man than Bertram Wooster would have warned her again about her blood pressure.

'I beg your pardon?' she said.

He repeated the key words.

'Oh?' said the relative, and went off with a pop. I could have told Upjohn he was asking for it. Normally as genial a soul as ever broke biscuit, this aunt, when stirred, can become the haughtiest of *grandes dames* before whose wrath the stoutest quail, and she doesn't, like some, have to use a lorgnette to reduce the citizenry to pulp, she does it all with the naked eye. 'Oh?' she said. 'So you have decided to revise my guest list for me? You have the nerve, the – the –'

I saw she needed helping out.

'Audacity,' I said, throwing her the line.

'The audacity to dictate to me who I shall have in my house.'

It should have been 'whom', but I let it go.

'You have the –'

'Crust.'

' – the immortal rind,' she amended, and I had to admit it was stronger, 'to tell me whom' – she got it right that time – 'I may entertain at Brinkley Court and who' – wrong again – 'I may not. Very well, if you feel unable to breathe the same air as my friends, you must please yourself. I believe the "Bull and Bush" in Market Snodsbury is quite comfortable.'

'Well spoken of in the *Automobile Guide*,' I said.

'I shall go there,' said Upjohn. 'I shall go there as soon as my things are packed. Perhaps you will be good enough to tell your butler to pack them.'

He strode off, and she went into Uncle Tom's study, me following, she still snorting. She rang the bell.

Jeeves appeared.

'Jeeves?' said the relative, surprised. 'I was ringing for –'

'It is Sir Roderick's afternoon off, madam.'

'Oh? Well, would you mind packing Mr Upjohn's things, Jeeves? He is leaving us.'

'Very good, madam.'

'And you can drive him to Market Snodsbury, Bertie.'

'Right-ho,' I said, not much liking the assignment, but liking less the idea of endeavouring to thwart this incandescent aunt in her current frame of mind.

Safety first, is the Wooster slogan.

19

It isn't much of a run from Brinkley Court to Market
Snodsbury and I deposited Upjohn at the 'Bull and Bush'
and started m.-p.-h.-ing homeward in what you might
call a trice. We parted, of course, on rather distant terms,
but the great thing when you've got an Upjohn on your
books is to part and not be fussy about how it's done,
and had it not been for all this worry about Kipper, for
whom I was now mourning in spirit more than ever, I
should have been feeling fine.

I could see no happy issue for him from the soup in
which he was immersed. No words had been exchanged
between Upjohn and self on the journey out, but the
glimpses I had caught of his face from the corner of the
eyes had told me that he was grim and resolute, his
supply of the milk of human kindness plainly short by
several gallons. No hope, it seemed to me, of turning
him from his fell purpose.

I garaged the car and went to Aunt Dahlia's sanctum
to ascertain whether she had cooled off at all since I had
left her, for I was still anxious about that blood pressure
of hers. One doesn't want aunts going up in a sheet of
flame all over the place.

She wasn't there, having, I learned later, withdrawn
to her room to bathe her temples with eau de Cologne
and do Yogi deep-breathing, but Bobbie was, and not
only Bobbie but Jeeves. He was handing her something
in an envelope, and she was saying 'Oh, Jeeves, you've
saved a human life,' and he was saying 'Not at all, miss.'
The gist, of course, escaped me, but I had no leisure to
probe into gists.

'Where's Kipper?' I asked, and was surprised to note that Bobbie was dancing round the room on the tips of her toes uttering animal cries, apparently ecstatic in their nature.

'Reggie?' she said, suspending the farmyard imitations for a moment. 'He went for a walk.'

'Does he know that Upjohn's found out he wrote that thing?'

'Yes, your aunt told him.'

'Then we ought to be in conference.'

'About Upjohn's libel action? It's all right about that. Jeeves has pinched his speech.'

I could make nothing of this. It seemed to me that the beasel spoke in riddles.

'Have you an impediment in your speech, Jeeves?'

'No, sir.'

'Then what, if anything, does the young prune mean?'

'Miss Wickham's allusion is to the typescript of the speech which Mr Upjohn is to deliver tomorrow to the scholars of Market Snodsbury Grammar School, sir.'

'She said you'd pinched it.'

'Precisely, sir.'

I started.

'You don't mean –'

'Yes, he does,' said Bobbie, resuming the Ballet Russe movements. 'Your aunt told him to pack Upjohn's bags, and the first thing he saw when he smacked into it was the speech. He trousered it and brought it along to me.'

I raised an eyebrow.

'Well, really, Jeeves!'

'I deemed it best, sir.'

'And did you deem right!' said Bobbie, executing a Nijinsky what-ever-it's-called. 'Either Upjohn agrees to drop that libel suit or he doesn't get these notes, as he calls them, and without them he won't be able to utter a word. He'll have to come across with the price of the papers. Won't he, Jeeves?'

'He would appear to have no alternative, miss.'

'Unless he wants to get up on that platform and stand there opening and shutting his mouth like a goldfish. We've got him cold.'

'Yes, but half a second,' I said.

I spoke reluctantly. I didn't want to damp the young ball of worsted in her hour of joy, but a thought had occurred to me.

'I see the idea, of course. I remember Aunt Dahlia telling me about this strange inability of Upjohn's to be silver-tongued unless he has the material in his grasp, but suppose he says he's ill and can't appear.'

'He won't.'

'I would.'

'But you aren't trying to get the Conservative Association of the Market Snodsbury division to choose you as their candidate at the coming by-election. Upjohn is, and it's vitally important for him to address the multitude tomorrow and make a good impression, because half the selection committee have sons at the school and will be there, waiting to judge for themselves how good he is as a speaker. Their last nominee stuttered, and they didn't discover it till the time came for him to dish it out to the constituents. They don't want to make a mistake this time.'

'Yes, I get you now,' I said. I remembered that Aunt Dahlia had spoken to me of Upjohn's political ambitions.

'So that fixes that,' said Bobbie. 'His future hangs on this speech, and we've got it and he hasn't. We take it from there.'

'And what exactly is the procedure?'

'That's all arranged. He'll be ringing up any moment now, making inquiries. When he does, you step to the telephone and outline the position of affairs to him.'

'Me?'

'That's right.'

'Why me?'

'Jeeves deems it best.'

'Well, really, Jeeves! Why not Kipper?'

'Mr Herring and Mr Upjohn are not on speaking terms, sir.'

'So you can see what would happen if he heard Reggie's voice. He would hang up haughtily, and all the weary work to do again. Whereas he'll drink in your every word.'

'But, dash it –'

'And, anyway, Reggie's gone for a walk and isn't available. I do wish you wouldn't always be so difficult, Bertie. Your aunt tells me it was just the same when you were a child. She'd want you to eat your cereal, and you would stick your ears back and be stubborn and non-co-operative, like Jonah's ass in the Bible.'

I could not let this go uncorrected. It's pretty generally known that when at school I won a prize for Scripture Knowledge.

'Balaam's ass. Jonah was the chap who had the whale. Jeeves!'

'Sir?'

'To settle a bet, wasn't it Balaam's ass that entered the *nolle prosequi*?'

'Yes, sir.'

'I told you so,' I said to Bobbie, and would have continued grinding her into the dust, had not the telephone at this moment tinkled, diverting my mind from the point at issue. The sound sent a sudden chill through the Wooster limbs, for I knew what it portended.

Bobbie, too, was not unmoved.

'Hullo!' she said. 'This, if I mistake not, is our client now. In you go, Bertie. Over the top and best of luck.'

I have mentioned before that Bertram Wooster, chilled steel when dealing with the sterner sex, is always wax in a woman's hands, and the present case was no

exception to the r. Short of going over Niagara Falls in a
barrel, I could think of nothing I wanted to do less than
chat with Aubrey Upjohn at this juncture, especially
along the lines indicated, but having been requested by
one of the delicately nurtured to take on the grim task, I
had no option. I mean, either a chap's *preux* or he isn't,
as the Chevalier Bayard used to say.

But as I approached the instrument and unhooked the
thing you unhook, I was far from being at my most
nonchalant, and when I heard Upjohn are-you-there-ing
at the other end my manly spirit definitely blew a fuse.
For I could tell by his voice that he was in the testiest of
moods. Not even when conferring with me at Malvern
House, Bramley-on-Sea, on the occasion when I put
sherbet in the ink, had I sensed in him a more marked
stirred-up-ness.

'Hullo? Hullo? Hullo? Are you there? Will you kindly
answer me? This is Mr Upjohn speaking.'

They always say that when the nervous system isn't
all it should be the thing to do is to take a couple of
deep breaths. I took six, which of course occupied a
certain amount of time, and the delay noticeably
increased his umbrage. Even at this distance one could
spot what I believe is called the deleterious animal
magnetism.

'Is that Brinkley Court?'

I could put him straight there. None other, I told him.

'Who are you?'

I had to think for a moment. Then I remembered.

'This is Wooster, Mr Upjohn.'

'Well, listen to me carefully, Wooster.'

'Yes, Mr Upjohn. How do you like the "Bull and
Bush"? Everything pretty snug?'

'What did you say?'

'I was asking if you like the "Bull and Bush".'

'Never mind the "Bull and Bush".'

'No, Mr Upjohn.'

'This is of vital importance. I wish to speak to the man who packed my things.'

'Jeeves.'

'What?'

'Jeeves.'

'What do you mean by Jeeves?'

'Jeeves.'

'You keep saying "Jeeves" and it makes no sense. Who packed my belongings?'

'Jeeves.'

'Oh, Jeeves is the man's name?'

'Yes, Mr Upjohn.'

'Well, he carelessly omitted to pack the notes for my speech at Market Snodsbury Grammar School tomorrow.'

'No, really! I don't wonder you're sore.'

'Saw whom?'

'Sore with an r.'

'What?'

'No, sorry. I mean with an o-r-e.'

'Wooster!'

'Yes, Mr Upjohn.'

'Are you intoxicated?'

'No, Mr Upjohn.'

'Then you are drivelling. Stop drivelling, Wooster.'

'Yes, Mr Upjohn.'

'Send for this man Jeeves immediately and ask him what he did with the notes for my speech.'

'Yes, Mr Upjohn.'

'At once! Don't stand there saying "Yes, Mr Upjohn".'

'No, Mr Upjohn.'

'It is imperative that I have them in my possession immediately.'

'Yes, Mr Upjohn.'

Well, I suppose, looking at it squarely, I hadn't made much real progress and a not too close observer might quite possibly have got the impression that I had lost my nerve and was shirking the issue, but that didn't in my opinion justify Bobbie at this point in snatching the receiver from my grasp and bellowing the word 'Worm!' at me.

'What did you call me?' said Upjohn.

'I didn't call you anything,' I said. 'Somebody called me something.'

'I wish to speak to this man Jeeves.'

'You do, do you?' said Bobbie. 'Well, you're going to speak to me. This is Roberta Wickham, Upjohn. If I might have your kind attention for a moment.'

I must say that, much as I disapproved in many ways of this carrot-topped Jezebel, as she was sometimes called, there was no getting away from it that she had mastered the art of talking to retired preparatory schoolmasters. The golden words came pouring out like syrup. Of course, she wasn't handicapped, as I had been, by having sojourned for some years beneath the roof of Malvern House, Bramley-on-Sea, and having at a malleable age associated with this old Frankenstein's monster when he was going good, but even so her performance deserved credit.

Beginning with a curt 'Listen, Buster,' she proceeded to sketch out with admirable clearness the salient points in the situation as she envisaged it, and judging from the loud buzzing noises that came over the wire, clearly audible to me though now standing in the background, it was evident that the nub was not escaping him. They were the buzzing noises of a man slowly coming to the realization that a woman's hand had got him by the short hairs.

Presently they died away, and Bobbie spoke.

'That's fine,' she said. 'I was sure you'd come round to our view. Then I will be with you shortly. Mind there's plenty of ink in your fountain pen.'

She hung up and legged it from the room, once more giving vent to those animal cries, and I turned to Jeeves as I had so often turned to him before when musing on the activities of the other sex.

'Women, Jeeves!'

'Yes, sir.'

'Were you following all that?'

'Yes, sir.'

'I gather that Upjohn, vowing . . . How does it go?'

'Vowing he would ne'er consent, consented, sir.'

'He's withdrawing the suit.'

'Yes, sir. And Miss Wickham prudently specified that he do so in writing.'

'Thus avoiding all rannygazoo?'

'Yes, sir.'

'She thinks of everything.'

'Yes, sir.'

'I thought she was splendidly firm.'

'Yes, sir.'

'It's the red hair that does it, I imagine.'

'Yes, sir.'

'If anyone had told me that I should live to hear Aubrey Upjohn addressed as "Buster" . . .'

I would have spoken further, but before I could get under way the door opened, revealing Ma Cream, and he shimmered silently from the room. Unless expressly desired to remain, he always shimmers off when what is called the Quality arrive.

20

This was the first time I had seen Ma Cream today, she having gone off around noon to lunch with some friends in Birmingham, and I would willingly not have seen her now, for something in her manner seemed to suggest that she spelled trouble. She was looking more like Sherlock Holmes than ever. Slap a dressing-gown on her and give her a violin, and she could have walked straight into Baker Street and no questions asked. Fixing me with a penetrating eye, she said:

'Oh, there you are, Mr Wooster. I was looking for you.'

'You wished speech with me?'

'Yes. I wanted to say that now perhaps you'd believe me.'

'I beg your pardon?'

'About that butler.'

'What about him?'

'I'll tell you about him. I'd sit down, if I were you. It's a long story.'

I sat down. Glad to, as a matter of fact, for the legs were feeling weak.

'You remember I told you I mistrusted him from the first?'

'Oh ah, yes. You did, didn't you?'

'I said he had a criminal face.'

'He can't help his face.'

'He can help being a crook and an impostor. Calls himself a butler, does he? The police could shake that story. He's no more a butler than I am.'

I did my best.

'But think of those references of his.'

'I am thinking of them.'

'He couldn't have stuck it out as major-domo to a man like Sir Roderick Glossop, if he'd been dishonest.'

'He didn't.'

'But Bobbie said –'

'I remember very clearly what Miss Wickham said. She told me he had been with Sir Roderick Glossop for years.'

'Well, then.'

'You think that puts him in the clear?'

'Certainly.'

'I don't, and I'll tell you why. Sir Roderick Glossop has a large clinic down in Somersetshire at a place called Chuffnell Regis, and a friend of mine is there. I wrote to her asking her to see Lady Glossop and get all the information she could about a former butler of hers named Swordfish. When I got back from Birmingham just now, I found a letter from her. She says that Lady Glossop told her she had never employed a butler called Swordfish. Try that one on for size.'

I continued to do my best. The Woosters never give up.

'You don't know Lady Glossop, do you?'

'Of course I don't, or I'd have written to her direct.'

'Charming woman, but with a memory like a sieve. The sort who's always losing one glove at the theatre. Naturally she wouldn't remember a butler's name. She probably thought all along it was Fotheringay or Binks or something. Very common, that sort of mental lapse. I was up at Oxford with a man called Robinson, and I was trying to think of his name the other day and the nearest I could get to it was Fosdyke. It only came back to me when I saw in *The Times* a few days ago that Herbert Robinson (26) of Grove Road, Ponder's End, had been had up at Bosher Street police court, charged with having stolen a pair of green and yellow checked trousers. Not the same chap, of course, but you get the idea. I've no doubt that one of these fine mornings Lady Glossop will suddenly smack herself on the forehead and cry "Swordfish! Of *course*! And all this time I've been thinking of the honest fellow as Catbird!"'

She sniffed. And if I were to say that I liked the way she sniffed, I would be wilfully deceiving my public. It was the sort of sniff Sherlock Holmes would have sniffed when about to clap the darbies on the chap who had swiped the Maharajah's ruby.

'Honest fellow, did you say? Then how do you account for this? I saw Willie just now, and he tells me that a valuable eighteenth-century cow-creamer which he bought from Mr Travers is missing. And where is it, you ask? At this moment it is tucked away in Swordfish's bedroom in a drawer under his clean shirts.'

In stating that the Woosters never give up, I was in error. These words caught me amidships and took all the fighting spirit out of me, leaving me a spent force.

'Oh, is it?' I said. Not good, but the best I could do.

'Yes, sir, that's where it is. Directly Willie told me the thing had gone, I knew where it had gone to. I went to this man Swordfish's room and searched it, and there it was. I've sent for the police.'

Again I had that feeling of having been spiritually knocked base over apex. I gaped at the woman.

'You've sent for the police?'

'I have, and they're sending a sergeant. He ought to be here at any moment. And shall I tell you something? I'm going now to stand outside Swordfish's door, to see that nobody tampers with the evidence. I'm not going to take any chances. I wouldn't want to say anything to suggest that I don't trust you implicitly, Mr Wooster, but I don't like the way you've been sticking up for this fellow. You've been far too sympathetic with him for my taste.'

'It's just that I think he may have yielded to sudden temptation and all that.'

'Nonsense. He's probably been acting this way all his life. I'll bet he was swiping things as a small boy.'

'Only biscuits.'

'I beg your pardon?'

'Or crackers you would call them, wouldn't you? He was telling me he occasionally pinched a cracker or two in his salad days.'

'Well, there you are. You start with crackers and you end up with silver jugs. That's life,' she said, and buzzed off to keep her vigil, leaving me kicking myself because I'd forgotten to say anything about the quality of mercy not being strained. It isn't, as I dare say you know, and a mention of this might just have done the trick.

I was still brooding on this oversight and wondering what was to be done for the best, when Bobbie and Aunt Dahlia came in, looking like a young female and an elderly female who were sitting on top of the world.

'Roberta tells me she has got Upjohn to withdraw the libel suit,' said Aunt Dahlia. 'I couldn't be more pleased, but I'm blowed if I can imagine how she did it.'

'Oh, I just appealed to his better feelings,' said Bobbie, giving me one of those significant glances. I got the message. The ancestor, she was warning me, must never learn that she had achieved her ends by jeopardizing the delivery of the Upjohn speech to the young scholars of Market Snodsbury Grammar School on the morrow. 'I told him that the quality of mercy . . . What's the matter, Bertie?'

'Nothing. Just starting.'

'What do you want to start for?'

'I believe Brinkley Court is open for starting in at about this hour, is it not? The quality of mercy, you were saying?'

'Yes. It isn't strained.'

'I believe not.'

'And in case you didn't know, it's twice bless'd and becomes the thronèd monarch better than his crown. I

drove over to the "Bull and Bush" and put this to
Upjohn, and he saw my point. So now everything's fine.'

I uttered a hacking laugh.

'No,' I said, in answer to a query from Aunt Dahlia. 'I
have not accidentally swallowed my tonsils, I was
merely laughing hackingly. Ironical that the young
blister should say that everything is fine, for at this very
moment disaster stares us in the eyeball. I have a story
to relate which I think you will agree falls into the
fretful porpentine class,' I said, and without further
pourparlers I unshipped my tale.

I had anticipated that it would shake them to their
foundation garments, and it did. Aunt Dahlia reeled like
an aunt struck behind the ear with a blunt instrument,
and Bobbie tottered like a red-haired girl who hadn't
known it was loaded.

'You see the set-up,' I continued, not wanting to rub it
in but feeling that they should be fully briefed. 'Glossop
will return from his afternoon off to find the awful
majesty of the Law waiting for him, complete with
handcuffs. We can hardly expect him to accept an
exemplary sentence without a murmur, so his first move
will be to establish his innocence by revealing all.
"True," he will say, "I did pinch this bally cow-creamer,
but merely because I thought Wilbert had pinched it and
it ought to be returned to store," and he will go on to
explain his position in the house – all this, mind you, in
front of Ma Cream. So what ensues? The sergeant
removes the gloves from his wrists, and Ma Cream asks
you if she may use your telephone for a moment, as she
wishes to call her husband on long distance. Pop Cream
listens attentively to the tale she tells, and when Uncle
Tom looks in on him later, he finds him with folded
arms and a forbidding scowl. "Travers," he says, "the
deal's off." "Off?" quivers Uncle Tom. "Off," says
Cream. "O-ruddy-double-f. I don't do business with guys
whose wives bring in loony-doctors to observe my son."

A short while ago Ma Cream was urging me to try something on for size. I suggest that you do the same for this.'

Aunt Dahlia had sunk into a chair and was starting to turn purple. Strong emotion always has this effect on her.

'The only thing left, it seems to me,' I said, 'is to put our trust in a higher power.'

'You're right,' said the relative, fanning her brow. 'Go and fetch Jeeves, Roberta. And what you do, Bertie, is get out that car of yours and scour the countryside for Glossop. It may be possible to head him off. Come on, come on, let's have some service. What are you waiting for?'

I hadn't exactly been waiting. I'd only been thinking that the enterprise had more than a touch of looking for a needle in a haystack about it. You can't find loony-doctors on their afternoon off just by driving around Worcestershire in a car; you need bloodhounds and handkerchiefs for them to sniff at and all that professional stuff. Still, there it was.

'Right-ho,' I said. 'Anything to oblige.'

21

And, of course, as I had anticipated from the start, the thing was a wash-out. I stuck it out for about an hour and then, apprised by a hollow feeling in the midriff that the dinner hour was approaching, laid a course for home.

Arriving there, I found Bobbie in the drawing-room. She had the air of a girl who was waiting for something, and when she told me that the cocktails would be coming along in a moment, I knew what it was.

'Cocktails, eh? I could do with one or possibly more,' I said. 'My fruitless quest has taken it out of me. I couldn't find Glossop anywhere. He must be somewhere, of course, but Worcestershire hid its secret well.'

'Glossop?' she said, seeming surprised. 'Oh, he's been back for ages.'

She wasn't half as surprised as I was. The calm with which she spoke amazed me.

'Good Lord! This is the end.'

'What is?'

'This is. Has he been pinched?'

'Of course not. He told them who he was and explained everything.'

'Oh, gosh!'

'What's the matter? Oh, of course, I was forgetting. You don't know the latest developments. Jeeves solved everything.'

'He did?'

'With a wave of the hand. It was so simple, really. One wondered why one hadn't thought of it oneself. On his advice, Glossop revealed his identity and said your aunt had got him down here to observe *you*.'

I reeled, and might have fallen, had I not clutched at a photograph on a near-by table of Uncle Tom in the uniform of the East Worcestershire Volunteers.

'*No?*' I said.

'And of course it carried immediate conviction with Mrs Cream. Your aunt explained that she had been uneasy about you for a long time, because you were always doing extraordinary things like sliding down water pipes and keeping twenty-three cats in your bedroom and all that, and Mrs Cream recalled the time when she had found you hunting for mice under her son's dressing-table, so she quite agreed that it was high time you were under the observation of an experienced eye like Glossop's. She was greatly relieved when Glossop assured her that he was confident of effecting a cure. She said we must all be very, very kind to you. So everything's nice and smooth. It's extraordinary how things turn out for the best, isn't it?' she said, laughing merrily.

Whether I would or would not at this juncture have taken her in an iron grasp and shaken her till she frothed is a point on which I can make no definite announcement. The chivalrous spirit of the Woosters would probably have restrained me, much as I resented that merry laughter, but as it happened the matter was not put to the test, for at this moment Jeeves entered, bearing a tray on which were glasses and a substantial shaker filled to the brim with the juice of the juniper berry. Bobbie drained her beaker with all possible speed and left us, saying that if she didn't get dressed, she'd be late for dinner, and Jeeves and I were alone, like a couple of bimbos in one of those movies where two strong men stand face to face and might is the only law.

'Well, Jeeves,' I said.

'Sir?'

'Miss Wickham has been telling me all.'

'Ah yes, sir.'

'The words "Ah yes, sir" fall far short of an adequate comment on the situation. A nice . . . what is it? Begins with an i . . . im-something.'

'Imbroglio, sir?'

'That's it. A nice imbroglio you've landed me in. Thanks to you . . .'

'Yes, sir.'

'Don't say "Yes, sir." Thanks to you I have been widely publicized as off my rocker.'

'Not widely, sir. Merely to your immediate circle now resident at Brinkley Court.'

'You have held me up at the bar of world opinion as a man who has not got all his marbles.'

'It was not easy to think of an alternative scheme, sir.'

'And let me tell you,' I said, and I meant this to sting, 'it's amazing that you got away with it.'

'Sir?'

'There's a flaw in your story that sticks up like a sore thumb.'

'Sir?'

'It's no good standing there saying "Sir?", Jeeves. It's obvious. The cow-creamer was in Glossop's bedroom. How did he account for that?'

'On my suggestion, sir, he explained that he had removed it from your room, where he had ascertained that you had hidden it after purloining it from Mr Cream.'

I started.

'You mean,' I . . . yes, thundered would be the word, 'You mean that I am now labelled not only as a loony in a general sort of way but also as a klept-whatever-it-is?'

'Merely to your immediate circle now resident at Brinkley Court, sir.'

'You keep saying that, and you must know it's the purest apple sauce. You don't really think the Creams will maintain a tactful reserve? They'll dine out on it for years. Returning to America, they'll spread the story from the rock-bound coasts of Maine to the Everglades of Florida, with the result that when I go over there again, keen looks will be shot at me at every house I go into and spoons counted before I leave. And do you realize that in a few shakes I've got to show up at dinner and have Mrs Cream being very, very kind to me? It hurts the pride of the Woosters, Jeeves.'

'My advice, sir, would be to fortify yourself for the ordeal.'

'How?'

'There are always cocktails, sir. Should I pour you another?'

'You should.'

'And we must always remember what the poet Longfellow said, sir.'

'What was that?'

'Something attempted, something done, has earned a night's repose. You have the satisfaction of having sacrificed yourself in the interests of Mr Travers.'

He had found a talking point. He had reminded me of those postal orders, sometimes for as much as ten bob, which Uncle Tom had sent me in the Malvern House days. I softened. Whether or not a tear rose to my eye, I cannot say, but it may be taken as official that I softened.

'How right you are, Jeeves!' I said.

The P G Wodehouse Society (UK)

The P G Wodehouse Society (UK) was formed in 1997 and exists to promote the enjoyment of the works of the greatest humorist of the twentieth century.

The Society publishes a quarterly magazine, *Wooster Sauce*, which features articles, reviews, archive material and current news. It also publishes an occasional newsletter in the *By The Way* series which relates a single matter of Wodehousean interest. Members are rewarded in their second and subsequent years by receiving a specially produced text of a Wodehouse magazine story which has never been collected into one of his books.

A variety of Society events are arranged for members including regular meetings at a London club, a golf day, a cricket match, a Society dinner, and walks round Bertie Wooster's London. Meetings are also arranged in other parts of the country.

Membership enquiries

Membership of the Society is available to applicants from all parts of the world. The cost of a year's membership in 1998 was £15. Enquiries and requests for an application form should be addressed in writing to the Membership Secretary, Christine Hewitt, at 26 Radcliffe Road, Croydon, Surrey CRO 5QE, or write to the Editor of *Wooster Sauce*, Tony Ring, at 34 Longfield, Great Missenden, Bucks HP16 OEG.

You can visit their website at:
http://www.eclipse.co.uk/wodehouse

Dr Arch
neurology

refresh yourself at penguin.co.uk

Visit penguin.co.uk for exclusive information and interviews with
bestselling authors, fantastic give-aways and the
inside track on all our books, from the Penguin Classics
to the latest bestsellers.

BE FIRST ▼

first chapters, first editions, first novels

EXCLUSIVES ▼

author chats, video interviews, biographies, special
features

EVERYONE'S A WINNER ▼

give-aways, competitions, quizzes, ecards

READERS GROUPS ▼

exciting features to support existing groups and
create new ones

NEWS ▼

author events, bestsellers, awards, what's new

EBOOKS ▼

books that click – download an ePenguin today

BROWSE AND BUY ▼

thousands of books to investigate – search, try
and buy the perfect gift online – or treat yourself!

ABOUT US ▼

job vacancies, advice for writers and company
history

Get Closer To Penguin . . . www.penguin.co.uk